Penny Tangey has published three humorous books for young people. Her most recent, *Stay Well Soon*, was shortlisted for the New South Wales and Western Australian Premier's awards and the Readings Children's Book Prize. Penny studied arts/science at Melbourne University, majoring in chemistry and Indonesian. While at university, Penny performed stand-up comedy, including in the Melbourne International Comedy Festival. Penny has worked as a researcher for television quiz shows *Hard Quiz* and *The Chase*, but she is still terrible at trivia. She is studying information management to become a librarian.

Also by Penny Tangey

Middle grade

Stay Well Soon

Young adult

Clara in Washington

Loving Richard Feynman

AS FAST AS I CAN
PENNY TANGEY
UQP

First published 2020 by University of Queensland Press
PO Box 6042, St Lucia, Queensland 4067 Australia
Reprinted 2020, 2022

University of Queensland Press (UQP) acknowledges the Traditional Owners and their custodianship of the lands on which UQP operates. We pay our respects to their Ancestors and their descendants, who continue cultural and spiritual connections to Country. We recognise their valuable contributions to Australian and global society.

uqp.com.au
reception@uqp.com.au

Cover design and illustration by Jo Hunt
Author photograph by Lincoln Turner
Typeset in 13/16 pt Minion Pro by Post Pre-press Group, Brisbane
Printed in Australia by McPherson's Printing Group

Australian Government | Australia Council for the Arts

The University of Queensland Press is assisted by the Australian Government through the Australia Council, its arts funding and advisory body.

A catalogue record for this book is available from the National Library of Australia.

ISBN 978 0 7022 6281 4 (pbk)
ISBN 978 0 7022 6408 5 (epdf)
ISBN 978 0 7022 6409 2 (epub)
ISBN 978 0 7022 6410 8 (kindle)

University of Queensland Press uses papers that are natural, renewable and recyclable products made from wood grown in well-managed forests and other controlled sources. The logging and manufacturing processes conform to the environmental regulations of the country of origin.

FSC www.fsc.org MIX Paper from responsible sources FSC® C001695

To my cousins

The important thing in life
is not the triumph, but the fight;
the essential thing is not to have won,
but to have fought well.

– Olympic creed

PART
ONE

1
TRAINING

I am going to the Olympics. Not just as a spectator because anyone can do that. I will be a competitor.

I haven't found out which sport I'm good at yet. Luckily, school sports day is in a few days. I can try different athletics events and find my talent.

Right now, I'm training. I'm standing next to the Hills hoist in our backyard about to do my first run-up for the long jump.

We don't have a regulation long jump pit, so I'm using the old sandpit. No one plays in it anymore and Mum hasn't got around to turning it into a vegetable garden. It took me ages to sift out the dead leaves and sticks from the sand so I won't get stabbed when I land.

I take a deep breath and mentally prepare myself.

I imagine the whole world watching on television. I hear the crowd cheering, see the flash of the cameras, Mum and Dad waving an Australian flag from their front row seats. I imagine the TV commentator saying, 'This is it for Vivian Hassler now. She needs a big jump to stay in the competition.'

I run as fast as I can. At the edge of the sandpit I jump, throwing my legs forward like I've seen in videos. I land on my bum in the sand. I think it was a legal jump, but I don't know how far I jumped because I don't have a tape measure.

Next, I'll try the triple jump. 'Hop, skip, jump. Hop, skip, jump,' I tell myself.

I set off for another good run-up, but unfortunately, I do the jump first instead of the skip and hop. I also pause for a long time and wobble between each bit, which is not how you're supposed to do it.

Never mind. I'll put it behind me.

On my next jump I get the hop and skip in the right order, but unfortunately, I trip over the edge of the sandpit and fall forward.

That's when I hear laughing. I turn around. Noah is leaning out of his bedroom window, watching the whole thing. I stand up quickly and get out of the sandpit.

'What are you trying to do, Vivian?' Noah calls out.

'Nothing!'

'Was that supposed to be the long jump?'

'No!'

'Well, what were you doing?'

'Nothing!' I run up the steps to the back door. The screen door slams shut behind me.

'Don't bang the door!' yells Mum from the kitchen. 'You'll give me a heart attack.'

Mum always thinks she's going to have a heart attack. She's a hypochondriac or something.

I go to my room and flop on my bed. I stare at the ceiling. Even though I know I'll compete at the Olympics, my family don't believe in me.

I'll show them. I will be the best at something, or at least the best in Australia. You can achieve anything you want if you work hard enough.

Maybe I'll win a medal as well.

I imagine myself on the podium, wearing a green and gold tracksuit, singing the Australian anthem.

I can't sit still.

I jump off the bed and go into the kitchen. 'Do I have time to go for a walk before tea?' I ask Mum.

'Not really, Viv. The rice is on.'

'Please? I'll be quick.'

'Okay. Fifteen minutes max.'

I bolt out the front door. I run down the driveway to the dirt road and sprint until my legs hurt and I'm puffed out. I slow down a little but keep running.

I imagine my TV interview after I win gold. I will thank my parents and my best friend, Olivia. Noah will feel so wrong for doubting me. He'll be interviewed and will say that I'm an inspiration to him, even though he's never achieved anything in his life. Actually, maybe it would be better if Noah becomes a world-famous trumpet player because then when he calls me an inspiration it will mean something.

I'm almost up to the main road. I look at my watch. I've been out for fifteen minutes. I'm going to be in trouble with Mum. I turn around and run faster back towards the house. Pretty soon my legs start to hurt again, but I still keep running.

By the time I get up to the Peterson's house I feel good. My feet thud against the ground while my heart beats fast. Tea will be ready and I'm late. I sprint the last 100 metres. I imagine the commentator shouting into the microphone, 'Vivian's lifting! She's overtaking! It's gold! Gold for Australia!'

At the gate I slow down and walk towards the house to get my breath back before I go inside. I pull my hairband out and my hair feels wet, almost like I've had a shower. I take a few deep breaths, and then I walk in the front door and into the kitchen. Tea is ready and everyone else is sitting at the table.

'Your face is bright red,' says Noah. 'You look like a tomato in a blonde wig.'

'Your face is bright white,' I say. 'You look like a fridge in a T-shirt.'

'Are you saying I'm fat?' asks Noah. His cheeks have gone a bit red too.

'I hope not, Vivian,' says Mum in her warning voice.

I wasn't saying he's the *size* of a fridge, just the colour of one, but now I feel confused. Why is it okay for him to call me a tomato in a wig but I can't say anything back?

'Anyway, not the point,' says Noah. 'What have you been doing?'

'I went for a walk.'

'Must have been a fast walk.'

'I know I should go for more fast walks,' says Dad, patting his tummy. He's pretty skinny, so it doesn't really make sense.

Noah rolls his eyes. Luckily Dad is looking at his plate, so he doesn't see Noah's bad attitude.

*

The next morning, I meet Olivia at the bottom of the hill before school as per usual.

Olivia and I have been best friends since prep and have always been in the same class. In grade two they were going to separate us, but then they didn't because of the fuss that happened. We're called *Olivian* because we're always together.

When I arrive, Olivia is jogging up and down on the spot. She's always cold because she always wears shorts, even in the middle of winter. Olivia asks how my training for school sports day is going. She is the only person who understands my Olympic dream.

'Okay,' I say.

'Which event are you concentrating on?' Olivia is side-skipping up the hill because it's very good for ankle strength. I have to walk fast to keep up with her.

'I dunno. What about you?'

'Sprinting, of course. I trained on the track for an hour last night.'

We measured out a 100-metre track in Olivia's backyard using a trundle wheel. Actually, it's only a 95-metre track because of the garage. Olivia is lucky to have that kind of training facility.

Olivia swaps sides and side-skips the other way, so now I'm looking at the back of her head. Her hair is only just long enough to tie in a ponytail, which is just a little black tuft sticking out of her hairband.

'I might set a new school record tomorrow as well as a personal best,' she calls out.

'What's your PB now?' I ask.

'I don't know.'

Olivia changes to walking backwards, which is very good for calf strength and balance. She doesn't need to look over her shoulder because she knows I'll tell her if she's going to hit anything.

'Does the school even keep records?' I ask.

'Alex will probably start this year. He's very professional.'

Alex is the new speciality PE teacher at Wallaby Flat Primary School. He's not just a PE teacher, but a former semi-professional athlete. We heard he once nearly went to the Commonwealth Games for marathon running, but then he didn't. We are so lucky Alex came to our school. Olivia and I want to show him that we're not like the other kids who are just mucking around. We have a future in sport.

'Anyway, you know we shouldn't do any more training now, right?' says Olivia.

'Really?'

'Yeah, we need to taper. You're supposed to stop training before a big event so you'll be well rested.'

Olivia has turned around now and is walking normally up the hill beside me.

'Of course,' I say. 'I'm tapering now. And we should carbo-load. I'm going to ask Mum to make vegetarian lasagne the night before school sports day.'

'I've heard that carbo-loading doesn't work,' says Olivia.

'But they're always going on about it in *Athletics World*.'

'Is that one of your dad's old sports magazines?'

I nod. Dad stopped subscribing in 2008. He blames having kids. The magazines are over ten years old, but I still find them interesting.

'Well, the science has moved on,' Olivia says. 'Last week I read an article that said eating lots of pasta before an event does more harm than good.'

'What are we supposed to eat then?'

'I don't know. Probably quinoa.'

'Are you going to have quinoa?'

'I doubt it.'

Olivia and I go to the classroom portable. Our teacher, Matt, is sitting at a desk with his laptop. He has shaved off his beard again. I don't know if he will ever make up his mind about it. Mum thinks he does it when he gets a new girlfriend.

‘Good morning, Olivian,’ he says without looking up from his computer.

‘Good morning, Matt,’ we say.

I put my bag in my locker just as the song that plays before the bell starts. Today the song is ‘When I Grow Up’ from the musical *Matilda*. It’s about what kids want to do when they grow up, but it doesn’t mention the Olympics, so I can’t really relate to it.

2
THE DREAM

I go to bed early, but I can't sleep. I think about school sports day. It's my chance to prove myself. I know it's a long way from school sports day to the Olympic Games, but a journey of 1000 miles starts with a single step, according to Olivia.

The 2016 Rio Olympics was probably the first step actually, because that's when I found my dream of becoming an elite athlete. I think the Olympics in Rio were the best ever, even if Australia didn't do as well in the pool as expected.

When Australia wins a gold medal it's really exciting. I'm glad I'm not from America or China – they win heaps of gold medals so it doesn't mean as much. Their athletes probably aren't even famous because there are so many other Olympic medallists – they are a dime a dozen in those places. In Australia, Olympic medallists are heroes because they're so rare, like hen's teeth.

I was in grade one during the Rio Olympics. At my house, we have a 'no screens before school' rule. The only exception is during the Olympics. When the Rio Olympics were on, I watched as much as I could.

I had a sleepover at Olivia's the night before the last day of the Olympics. Olivia's family don't usually watch sport, but they have a rule that the visitor gets to choose the TV show. I chose the Olympics, and that night the pentathlon was on.

The commentators did a lot of explaining about the pentathlon because most people have never heard of it until the Olympics. The modern pentathlon has five parts: fencing, swimming, riding horses, shooting targets with lasers, and running. The commentator said the person who invented the modern pentathlon chose those events because they were like fighting a war in the olden days.

Olivia and I started watching when they were up to the last stage of the pentathlon. The athletes had to do a three-kilometre run and stop along the way to shoot at targets with a laser gun, just like in a war, I guess.

At first Olivia wasn't very interested. She was stencilling and not paying attention. Then the commentators got very excited because the Australian athlete, Chloe Esposito, was running and shooting really well. She started in seventh place, but she was catching up.

When Chloe Esposito got to the final target, Olivia put down her pencils. We both lay on our stomachs watching. Chloe Esposito made her shots before any of the other competitors and took off for the final run leg.

Olivia and I jumped up and down and cheered.

All Chloe Esposito needed to do was run 800 metres to the finish. No one could catch her.

When she crossed the finish line, she grabbed the tape and held it above her head. She didn't look happy, she looked fierce, then shocked. Later, when she got her gold medal, she couldn't stop smiling and you could tell it was a dream come true.

That night I told Olivia I wanted to go to the Olympics when I grow up. Olivia said she did too. So that was final – we decided to go together.

Olivia knew straight away that she wanted to be a sprinter because she was inspired by the end of Chloe Esposito's race.

I wasn't sure what my event would be.

The next day, Olivia and I got up at six in the

morning and snuck out of her room to watch more Olympics. It was the final day and the men's marathon was on.

Olivia and I both agreed that 41 kilometres is way too far to run. It's almost halfway to Echuca!

The men's marathon takes ages, so while it was on they also showed highlights from other events at the games, like Simone Biles winning all the medals in the gymnastics. She's from America, but she was still inspirational.

'You could do that,' said Olivia.

I wasn't sure because flipping over backwards looked scary.

Back at the men's marathon, a Kenyan runner named Eliud Kipchoge won the race. He was a long way in front of the others, so it wasn't that exciting. I noticed that some of the runners looked okay when they were running, but as soon as they finished, they looked exhausted, like they could barely walk. They had given everything they had.

In the car home from Olivia's house, I asked Mum and Dad if they remembered the Sydney Olympics.

Mum laughed. 'Yes. I do.'

'Olivia's parents didn't get to go because they were living in Indonesia then,' I say. 'What events did you and Dad go to?'

‘We didn’t actually go either,’ said Mum.

‘We were living in Melbourne then,’ said Dad.

‘It’s not that far to Sydney.’

‘Yeah, but it was very expensive. I was studying. We couldn’t afford it,’ said Dad.

I couldn’t believe Mum and Dad missed their chance, and they didn’t even seem to regret it. ‘Do you remember anything about the Olympics?’ I asked.

Dad nodded. ‘Sure, I remember Cathy Freeman winning the 400 metres. We went to the pub to watch it.’

‘It was very exciting,’ said Mum. ‘When she won everyone in the pub cheered and jumped up and down.’

‘Some people cried,’ said Dad.

‘Why did people cry?’ I asked.

‘They were happy.’

‘Cathy Freeman must have been so happy.’

‘I think she was mainly relieved,’ said Mum.

‘Definitely,’ says Dad. ‘The pressure must have been so intense.’

‘I’d love to do it!’ I said. ‘It would be the best.’ I told Mum and Dad that Olivia and I are going to the Olympics, Olivia as a sprinter and me doing something else.

‘The important thing is to find a sport you

enjoy,' said Dad.

'I'll definitely enjoy going to the Olympics.'

'I think I wanted to go to the Olympics,' said Dad. 'I was good at hurdling in school.'

'What happened?'

'I wasn't good enough,' said Dad.

'Oh. Never mind.' I felt bad for Dad, but it's too late for him. 'So, can I do gymnastics?'

'We'll see.'

I didn't give up and eventually 'we'll see' became 'yes'.

One afternoon, about two years later, I got home from gymnastics and cried and cried. The gymnastics teacher said she pushed us hard to get results, but after nearly two years of classes I still wasn't getting results. I fell off the beam twenty times that lesson, and Pat, the gym coach, told me to go sit on the bench.

As I walked towards the side of the room, one of the girls called out, 'Don't fall off!'

Even Pat laughed.

That's why I cried and cried when I got home.

Mum came into my room. 'Sweetie, you know you don't have to keep going to gymnastics if you don't want to?'

'But I want to.'

'It's just that Pat told me you spend most of the class looking scared.'

'It's only because I'm nervous of heights. I don't like being up on the bar, or the vault, or the uneven bars. And I'm worried I'll break my back when I do flips and stuff. And I can't understand why I can't touch my toes because I stretch *all the time*.'

Mum sat beside me on my bed. 'It doesn't sound like much fun. You can stop, you know.'

'I CAN'T.'

'But why not?'

'I want to go to the Olympics,' I mumbled into my pillow. I had to repeat it twice before Mum heard.

'Sweetie, Viv – I don't think you're going to be an Olympic gymnast.'

Normally talking to Mum makes me feel better, but that night I cried myself to sleep because I realised that Mum didn't believe in my Olympic dream.

Olivia convinced me not to give up. She said there were heaps of other sports – we just needed to find my talent.

So last winter I joined a soccer team. I went to two training sessions. I practised in the backyard with a soccer ball and turned the trampoline over to make a goal. At my first proper game of soccer I only kicked the ball once, and that was in the wrong direction. I got yelled at by my teammates.

Nana was visiting and came to watch, and she laughed her head off. Later, she tried to say she was coughing, but I know what I saw.

I didn't waste time like I had with gymnastics. I quit soccer straight away. In fact, Olivia and I ruled out all ball sports to be efficient.

Dad was disappointed because he says team sports teach good values. That's one of the reasons he was so mad at Noah when he refused to play football last season. He thinks Noah won't have good values now.

That's all fine, but I don't have time for values. I need to find my talent.

Next, I tried swimming. Susie Maroney came to our school at the end of the year and gave a talk about how she achieved her dreams. She didn't go to the Olympics, but she's a long-distance swimmer who swam across the English Channel covered in butter and beat the record. She has cerebral palsy, but she didn't let that stop her. She told us that if you have a passion and you work hard enough, you can achieve anything you want to.

I did swimming lessons in the summer holidays

and I worked super hard. I did lots of laps and learned to breathe on both sides because Jill, our swimming coach, said proper swimmers can breathe on both sides.

When I'm trying to swim fast, I worry about drowning. When I get puffed out, I imagine being trapped under water holding my breath until I can't stand it. I try to gasp, and then my lungs fill with water. I imagine struggling and then floating face-down in the water.

At the school swimming carnival, I entered all the races, but I came seventh in every single one, even backstroke, which Jill said was my strong suit.

I was very disappointed with my results. Mum said consistency takes a special kind of talent, but there's no Olympic event for people who are excellent at coming second last.

Kim, the grade six teacher and house leader of the You Yangs team, told me to remember my good sportspersonship or I wouldn't be allowed to swim in the relay team.

I stopped complaining after that. I swam the second leg of the relay and Olivia also swam second for her team, the Dandenongs.

We both dived into the water at almost the same time. I tried so hard to keep up with Olivia and she was only a little bit in front when we finished the first lap. I did a tumble turn, even though I was scared of hitting my head. Tumble turns are non-negotiable for Olympic swimmers. I was trying so hard to beat Olivia, but I messed up the tumble turn like I'd always worried about, even though Jill said, 'Stop carrying on like a pork chop, Vivian. You're not going to hit your head!'

The next thing I remember I was being pulled out of the pool. I coughed up a bit of water. Lots of kids were crowding around and Kim was yelling at them to get back on the grassy area. An ambulance came and took me to hospital. I was in hospital overnight while they checked that my brain was okay. They didn't find anything wrong with me. I just had a bad headache.

Olivia and her mum came to visit me in hospital. Olivia gave me a silver balloon with 'Get Well Soon' on it. She told me that Alex jumped into the deep end wearing his clothes and pulled me out, but I don't remember that. Apparently, his T-shirt went see-through.

Back at school, a boy in my class named Daniel kept saying, 'Who am I? Who am I?' and pretending to get knocked out and drown. Daniel is funny sometimes and annoying the rest of the time. I didn't think it was funny because I could have died if Alex hadn't rescued me.

You can achieve anything if you work hard enough. But I decided it would be easier to work hard at something I'm not really bad at.

Finding out I couldn't be an Olympic swimmer was particularly disappointing because it meant I couldn't compete in pentathlon, triathlon, synchronised swimming or water polo either.

Olivia and I brainstormed other options but we kept hitting roadblocks. I begged Mum and Dad to let me do archery or shooting because I almost always get my apple cores in the compost bin when I throw them from the kitchen doorway. But Mum said no child of hers would hold a gun, and archery gives her the shivers. Same for fencing.

Olivia suggested the Winter Olympics might be an option, but I've only been to the snow once. I didn't like it because I got very cold and then I got chilblains, which are sore and itchy red bumps, on my toes. Anyway, we're a long way from the snow in Bendigo, so there are very few winter sport training opportunities.

Equestrian was out of the question, according to Dad. He said I should focus on something cheap and close, like running.

The problem is, even though I like running, I'm not good enough at it. When we have races at school, Olivia always wins and I come second. If I'm not even the best in our school, I definitely won't be the best in Australia.

That's why the school sports day tomorrow is so important. I will try three new Olympic sports – long jump, triple jump and high jump. One of them *has* to be my talent.

I need to find my talent soon because the 2032 Olympics are only twelve years away. Brisbane has put in a bid to host the 2032 Olympics, and it would be amazing to compete in front of a home crowd. Indonesia has also put in a bid for Jakarta in 2032. I would be happy for them to win for two reasons: 1. Olivia has family who live in Jakarta, so that would be really special for her, and 2. I would like to go overseas. Also, the Olympic Games have never been held in Indonesia, so it would be more fair. That's three reasons, not two. I must be getting tired.

I imagine the opening ceremony of the Olympic Games. The roar of the crowd as I walk into the stadium behind the Australian flag. The Australian team's uniform will be green pants, a gold tracksuit top and a silver Akubra. I will keep the Akubra to show my grandchildren, even though I'm pretty sure I don't ever want to have children because it is gross, but I'll keep it anyway, just in case I adopt.

3

SCHOOL SPORTS DAY

It's still dark at five-thirty when I wake up on school sports day. I shut my eyes and try to go back to sleep. Being well rested will help me perform at my peak. Although *Athletics World* says that sleep before training is more important than sleep before events because the adrenaline on the big day carries you through. Whereas, you can't train a tired body, apparently.

Although maybe this isn't true. Maybe the science has moved on like with carbo-loading.

Last night I asked Mum if we could have quinoa for tea, but she said no because she doesn't have time for ancient grains and what's wrong with rice or couscous? She put cashews in the stir-fry for extra protein, but I don't think they were activated cashews. I've only had activated nuts once. They tasted a bit wet, but maybe that's how you know they're working.

Lying in bed with my eyes closed is hopeless. I'm not going back to sleep.

I'm not allowed to get up before six so I do my stretches as quietly as I can in my room. I stretch my hamstrings, calves and quads and then I do shoulder rolls. By the end I feel less stiff, but I still can't touch my toes.

I put on my normal school uniform, which is blue shorts and a green T-shirt. Then I tie a yellow ribbon in my hair to show which team I'm in.

Someone is moving around in the kitchen, which means I can finally go out for breakfast.

Mum is standing at the kitchen bench dressed in her work uniform. Technically she can wear whatever she wants to work, but she always wears black pants and a boring shirt. Mum's already laid out bread for sandwiches on the kitchen bench.

'I don't need a sandwich today, remember?' I say. 'There's going to be a sausage sizzle.'

'Why?'

'For SCHOOL SPORTS DAY.'

'Of course. I've got the board meeting this afternoon, unfortunately. Dad's going to come.'

I look in the cupboard and think about what

to eat. Quinoa-Bix would be ideal, obviously, but we don't have those. I get out Weet-Bix as per usual. I put one Weet-Bix in my bowl and pour on milk. I eat it and put another one in the bowl. I always eat them one at a time so they don't go soggy. I have a third Weet-Bix because you can't perform at your peak when you're hungry.

Mum goes to Noah's room to tell him to come and have breakfast. Ever since he started year nine, Noah has lacked self-motivation and discipline, according to Dad. He also says that Mum mollycoddles Noah and lets him get away with too much.

When Noah finally makes it to the kitchen, he's still in his pyjamas, which are definitely too small for him now. He's also annoyed because there's no Nutri-Grain. I don't know why he's surprised – we never have Nutri-Grain except one box as a treat during the school holidays, and when it's gone, it's gone.

'I hate Weet-Bix,' Noah says. 'They taste like cardboard.'

Dad walks into the kitchen. 'Nutri-Grain tastes like type 2 diabetes,' he says.

'By which you mean delicious,' says Noah.

'You may as well have a milkshake for breakfast.'

'Well, if you're offering, that would be great.'

'Noah, have toast if you don't want Weet-Bix,' says Mum. She sits opposite me at the table with her coffee.

Dad brings his muesli and sits beside me. 'You ready for the big day?'

'Kind of.'

'I hope you don't fall flat on your face again,' says Noah.

'Shut up.'

'At least Vivian is having a go,' says Dad. 'Having a go is what counts.'

Going to the Olympics is what counts, but I don't say anything because at least Dad is sticking up for me. Dad encourages me, even if he doesn't believe I will make the Olympic team. That's why I'll dedicate my first autobiography to him and maybe Mum, but not Noah.

Noah mutters something under his breath.

'What was that, Noah?' says Dad.

'Nothing.'

'I heard you say something.'

'Let it go,' says Mum.

I hate it when she says that. Now I'll have the song stuck in my head for the rest of the day.

'Oh, by the way,' says Dad. 'Nana can't make it today.'

'I didn't know she was thinking of coming,' I say.

Secretly, I feel a bit relieved because Nana never takes sport seriously, which can be annoying.

'She wanted to,' says Dad. 'But she's been called out unexpectedly to yarn bomb a music festival.'

'Really?' says Mum, standing up from the table.

'Yeah, I think it's a CWA thing,' says Dad. 'Have you had breakfast?' he asks Mum.

'No. I'm not hungry.'

'Food is fuel,' I say because if I have read that once in *Athletics World*, I have read it a thousand times.

'Do you eat petrol?' Noah says.

I ignore Noah because he knows nothing about nutrition. 'Have a Weet-Bix,' I say to Mum.

'Or some wood. Tastes the same,' says Noah. 'Good for fuel, good for you, that's what I always say.'

He never says that.

Dad drives me to school and drops me at the bottom of the hill. He's going to work on his laptop in the café near school and come back when school sports day starts. As I get out of the car, he says, 'Remember, just to do your best, and have fun.'

Olivia is crouching on the grass, doing stretches for her problem Achilles tendon. 'How do you feel?' she asks as I sit down beside her.

'Okay. How are you?'

'Nervous.'

'I don't think it's fair that we have to do maths first,' I say as I stretch my legs out too. 'The whole day should be sports.' I lean forward and just manage to touch my ankles.

'At least it will give us something else to think about.'

I don't know how Olivia can think about maths at a time like this.

'Did you sleep well?' asks Olivia.

'Not really. I woke up early. And it took me ages to get to sleep last night.'

'Try not to worry about it.' Olivia stands up and stretches her arms above her head.

'I'm so nervous,' I say, standing up too.

'So am I. This might be the most important day of our lives.'

Olivia gets it. School sports day is not just about *having fun.*

I don't like maths at the best of times, but on sports day it's even harder to concentrate on probability.

We have to roll dice and write down which numbers come up. Olivia and I work together. There's a lot of chatter and Matt gives us some warnings, but it's only a matter of time before

Kim comes in from the classroom next door to complain. Although the grade sixes can't talk, because when they practise recorder the noise is horrific.

Matt is standing at the front of the room with his hand up. I nudge Olivia, who is under the table trying to find our dice again. She sits back on her chair and looks at Matt. The rest of the class is quietening down too.

'Okay,' says Matt. 'I get that everyone's excited about sports day. So, let's do something different.'

Unfortunately, Matt keeps writing numbers on the board, and it turns out that the 'something different' is still going to be maths.

Matt says, 'If there are eight people in a 200-metre sprint, what is the chance that the runner in lane four wins the race?'

Calvin puts his hand up and says, 'One in eight.'

'That's right,' says Matt. 'And looking at our probability line, where would you say one chance in eight sits?' He points to the probability line that says: Impossible, Unlikely, Possible, Even Chance, Likely, Very Likely, Certain.

I put my hand up and Matt picks me. 'Possible,' I say.

'Yeah, I think that's right,' says Matt. 'Now let's change the question slightly. How would you rate the chance if Usain Bolt is running in lane four and the other competitors are your parents?'

Olivia says, 'Usain Bolt would definitely win. So, it's Certain.'

Matt agrees. 'I would say that it is close enough to Certain. And how would you rate the chance of your parents in the race against Usain Bolt.'

'Impossible!' everyone else shouts.

I don't think it's impossible, though. You can achieve anything if you work hard enough and have a dream.

We go outside for recess where preparations for sports day are underway. The barbeque is set up on the basketball court. Last night someone spray-painted a running track on the grass on the oval. In the middle of the oval, areas for different sports are marked out with flags. Some spectators are arriving and Faye, the school principal, is directing people.

I'm too nervous to be hungry but I make myself eat a muesli bar for morning tea because food is fuel, even if Noah doesn't believe me. Olivia has some crackers. We don't talk much because we're so focussed.

When the song starts for the end of recess, Olivia and I look at each other.

‘This is it, Olivian,’ she says.

My stomach turns over again. I don’t think I’ve ever felt this nervous.

We walk to the oval together then split up to assemble in our house teams. Today all the teachers are wearing high-vis vests, like they’re all on yard duty.

I’m in the You Yangs, the yellow house. Olivia is in Dandenongs, the blue house. I don’t mind being in a different house to Olivia. I know we’re both on Team Olivian.

The grade six teacher, Kim, is the house leader for the You Yangs. She marks us You Yangs off the roll, then tells us what the schedule is.

Grade fives are doing the sandbag toss first. This is a replacement for shotput, which we’re not allowed to do because it’s not practical for everyone to wear helmets at all times. There’s only one other girl from my class in the You Yangs, a new kid named Liza.

Liza stands out in our class because she’s the shortest, the only kid with glasses, and the only kid with red hair. She started at our school last week, so this is her first school sports day. She used to go to school in Melbourne. On her first day she wore the uniform from her old school, which was a purple-and-white checked dress. No one at my school ever wears a dress. Now Liza's wearing a green polo top with blue shorts like everyone else, but you can still tell she's new because her top is such a bright green.

Liza and I walk to the sandbag toss together. I ask Liza if she's nervous, but she says she isn't. I guess she doesn't care about sport. Some people are like that.

A few parents are standing around chatting in the spectators' area. My dad hasn't arrived yet but that's okay. The sandbag toss is not a very important event. It's not even an Olympic sport, just a safer version of shotput. There is no safe alternative to javelin, sadly.

Principal Faye is in charge of the sandbag toss, and she explains the rules. The tosser stands in a circle and spins around before hurling the sandbag as far as possible.

Everyone in the class gets one throw and the top six will go through to the final.

Liza goes first. I give her a big clap and cheer because she is a You Yang. She spins around and around like a twister and throws as hard as she can. The sandbag soars through the air, but unfortunately it lands outside the white line. It's an illegal throw and Liza won't get through to the next round. She shrugs and doesn't look upset at all.

Calvin is the first boy to throw, and it is embarrassingly bad.

Next is Olivia. She only spins around a couple of times but the sandbag flies in a high arc, rotating as it soars through the air before it finally plonks to the ground inside the white lines. That throw will be hard to beat.

The crowd goes wild. Well, everyone claps.

I get more and more nervous watching everyone else have their turn. When it finally gets to me, I feel sick. I pick up a sandbag and am surprised at how heavy it is. From what I've seen, spinning around too many times makes you throw the sandbag in the wrong direction. So, I rotate once and then let the sandbag go.

Unfortunately, the bag slips awkwardly from my hand, and instead of soaring into the air it lands with a plunk a couple of metres *behind me.* I've thrown a negative distance.

Kids laugh and someone in the spectators' area snorts.

'Never mind, You Yangs!' Liza shouts. 'Better luck next time!' She has a surprisingly loud voice for someone so little.

I know there won't be a next time because I have no chance of making round two of the sandbag toss. I was worse than Calvin.

It's all Matt's fault. The other classes have been practising events for school sports day, but Matt's grade five is all maths, maths, maths.

Olivia wins the sandbag toss. She gets a blue ribbon. Nasrin comes second and Sam comes third. I get a purple ribbon, but so does everyone who participated – even Calvin. You don't get any house points for a purple ribbon. Sam gets one point for coming third; Nasrin two points for coming second; and Olivia gets three whole points for winning.

Olivia walks beside me and whispers in my ear, 'Three points for Team Olivian!'

That makes me smile.

Our next event is the high jump. I am very nervous because I've only practised the high jump once before, and it didn't go very well. The crashmat also reminds me of gymnastics, which doesn't help my confidence.

Kim is in charge of the high jump and she shows us how to take a run-up in a curved line and scissor kick over the bar. She makes it look easy. Kim tells us that Fosbury flops *are banned* because of last year. If anyone deliberately lands on their back, they will be disqualified. One of the main aims of this year's school sports day, according to Kim, is to get through the whole day without calling an ambulance.

Unlike in the Olympics, we only get two chances at each bar height because otherwise we'd be here all day. It's a brutal way to run the competition.

We line up and I'm near the back.

Sam goes first. He makes it look easy as he runs in a wide arc and jumps over the bar landing on his feet on the soft mat. He does a somersault in the air when he jumps off the mat and Kim gives him a warning.

Holly is next. Her run-up is okay, but she stops when she gets to the bar like a spooked horse in an equestrian event.

Olivia does a great jump, of course. She kicks elegantly over the bar like it's the easiest thing in the world. A familiar voice says, 'Great work, Olivia!' and I turn and see it's my dad barracking for her.

Olivia walks by on her way back from the mat. 'Remember to approach the bar with confidence,' she whispers to me.

I watch the rest of the class. Lots of people don't approach the bar with confidence and knock it down, like Liza. Or they stop like Holly, or fall over like Calvin.

When it's my turn I follow the same path as Olivia's run-up, making sure I'm confident as I approach. But I reach the bar at the wrong angle and I'm confused about which leg should scissor over first. I jump and kick my legs, but I don't have enough height and I crash sideways into the bar and onto the mat. I land on the bar, which hurts my ribs, but I am not going to cry.

Daniel yells out, 'Slitherin' Vivian!'

'Are you okay, Vivian?' Kim calls out.

I nod and sit up before sliding off the mat. I am not going to cry.

'Don't worry about the others,' Kim says. 'At least you had a go.'

Kim turns to the rest of the class. 'Everyone, we're all here to try and do our best. If I hear anyone else laughing, they will be disqualified. We will not tolerate bad sportspersonship.'

I look over at my dad and he smiles at me and shrugs. I am not going to cry.

I walk back to the group, trying not to look at anyone, but I accidentally catch Sam's eye and he smiles at me.

In the end, only Sam and Olivia are left in the high jump competition. Sam is shorter than Olivia, but he can jump really high. Kim raises the bar three more times. Finally, Olivia knocks the bar over on her first attempt. On her second attempt she just clips the bar with her foot as she jumps over. It wobbles. It falls.

Sam clears that height, so Olivia gets a red ribbon for high jump, Sam gets a blue and I get another purple. I say congratulations to Sam, and he says thank you because he has very good manners, according to Mum.

It's time for lunch. I line up with Dad and Olivia for a sausage from the sausage sizzle.

'Great work, Olivia!' says Dad. '*Bagus sekali.*'

Dad learned Indonesian when he was at university and he's always dropping in phrases when he speaks to Olivia. It's embarrassing, but I can't stop him.

'Thanks,' says Olivia.

'I thought you had him with the high jump. You were a bit unlucky, I think.'

Olivia shrugs. 'Next time.'

'She won the sandbag toss,' I say.

'How did you go in that?' Dad asks me.

'I got purple.'

'Not to worry,' says Dad, then adds, '*Tidak apa-apa*.' He looks really proud of himself, even though he's just said the same thing twice and Olivia obviously doesn't need a translator.

'Well, the sandbag toss and the high jump weren't my main events. I'm focussing on the long jump.'

'Just take it one event at a time,' says Olivia.

'Good advice,' says Dad.

Principal Faye writes the scores on the board. The You Yangs are coming last behind the Grampians and Dandenongs.

Team Olivian has five points, but that's not cheering me up anymore.

After lunch, it's finally time for the grade five long jump competition. This time I make sure I'm first in line because waiting makes me nervous.

Our class teacher, Matt, is in charge of the long jump, and he looks really bored. He gives me the signal and I run as fast as I can. When I hit the white mark, I jump and throw myself forward. I land in the sand.

'Great jump!' yells a spectator who sounds like my dad.

My sandpit training is finally paying off. Matt examines the sand and measures my jump. That should make him happy because he's always making us measure things in maths.

Olivia is next and she jumps a metre further than I did.

I will not let it rattle me. I know I can improve.

Calvin goes next. He isn't running very fast when he gets to the line. Daniel is lining up after me and he says, 'Calvin runs like a girl', which makes a few kids laugh but not me. Calvin's jump barely gets him into the pit. He lands on his bum and struggles to get out of the soft sand. Matt helps him up and Daniel calls Calvin a beached whale. Daniel should be disqualified for bad sportspersonship.

On my next turn, I sprint towards the line. When I launch into the air, I'm flying. I land in the sand and stand up. I think I've beaten my personal best, and maybe jumped further than Olivia.

I'm grinning when I notice Matt's sympathetic face. 'Sorry, Vivian,' he says. 'That was an illegal jump.'

'What do you mean?'

'Your foot was over the line.'

'No, it wasn't!'

'It was so too, Slitherin' Vivian!' says Daniel.

I look at Olivia, hoping she will back me up, but she is looking at the ground. So much for Team Olivian.

I'm allowed to have another jump but this time I don't run as fast and I don't jump as far. I'm out of the competition.

I sit next to Liza with the other spectators. She seems to be in a good mood, even though she's out too. 'Olivia is so good at sport!' says Liza.

'Yeah,' I say because it's true. I pick up a piece

of grass and rip it into little pieces. 'I'm bad at everything.'

There's a long pause and then Liza says, 'I bet you're good at lots of things.'

'Like what?' I say.

'You did pretty well in the spelling last week. Weren't you second best in the class?'

'Who cares about spelling!'

'Calvin.'

She's right. He's the best speller in the class and it's pretty important to him.

'And the teachers care too,' adds Liza.

'True,' I say. I smile at Liza. I don't exactly feel better, but I appreciate her trying.

Olivia does her final jump and beats Sam. Another blue ribbon for Olivia and another three points for her team.

In the triple jump I fall over after the hop, during the skip and before the jump. Olivia wins again. She gets her *third* blue ribbon. I have four purples. Olivia has won eleven house points. I haven't won any.

Here's a maths problem: What's the probability of me winning against Olivia? Zero.

4

BEST SPORTSPERSON

We go to the track next, where Alex is waiting for the sprints. Olivia is so excited. Even though she already has three blue ribbons she wants more. 'This is our chance to show Alex our real potential,' Olivia says. 'Go Team Olivian!'

This time everyone isn't participating together. We're split into two groups: boys and girls.

The first race is the boys' 100 metres. During Calvin's heat, Daniel points at him and says, 'Here comes the girly runner!'

I wish Daniel would fall over in his race, but he doesn't. He wins, and then he gets to run in the final. Sam and Daniel are heaps faster than all the other boys. It is a close race between them. Daniel's dad is screaming at him to go faster.

When Sam crosses the finish line just in front, Daniel's dad swears, but I am really pleased.

It's the girls' turn next. There are twelve girls in grade five, so we will have two heats of six and the top four runners from each heat will go into the final. I'm feeling nervous again. I want to run as fast as I can. Even if there's no chance of beating Olivia, I'm going to show Daniel that girls can run fast too.

Our school doesn't have a proper starter's gun, so Alex says, 'On your marks'. Pause. 'Set.' Pause. This is taking forever. 'Go!'

We take off. Olivia is out in front but I'm not worried because Holly and Corrie aren't trying. So I don't run my fastest. Olivia wins the heat by a very long way. I coast home and come fourth.

For the final, Olivia is in the lane next to me. Our school doesn't own starting blocks so we stand in our lanes waiting.

I hear Dad yell, 'Go, You Yangs!'

I shake my legs and rotate my arms a few times. I look down the track to the finish line. I block out the noise of our class and the parents talking. I stare at the grass between the white lines on the oval and concentrate on what I need to do.

Finally, it's time. 'On your marks!' says Alex. 'Set. Go!'

I take off. Olivia is way ahead of me. She must have jumped the gun, but Alex doesn't call a false start.

I run. My legs rotate faster, and I pump my arms like the sprinters do in the Olympics, but Olivia is in front and I don't get any closer to her. I notice that Nasrin is running almost beside me. We are ten metres from the finish. *Not this time, Nasrin*, I think, and push myself forward, throwing myself across the line, just in front of her. I've come second! A podium finish at last, except that our school doesn't own a podium.

Dad is clapping and cheering for me, not just for Olivia this time.

Liza finishes just after me. 'Congratulations!' she says. Then she adds, 'You see, you're not bad at everything. Second in spelling AND running!'

I get a red ribbon and two points, but there's no time to celebrate because we have one last race – the 400 metres.

This race is optional so there are no heats. Some people like Holly don't understand that you have to be in it to win it, and they don't want to race.

Olivia is in the outside lane so she starts a long way in front. In our maths class, Matt explained how staggered starts work, so I know Olivia will run the exact same distance as me. Looking at her now though, it feels like she's impossibly far ahead, like I'll never catch up to her. Next to Olivia is Liza and then Nasrin and then it's me in a middle lane.

'On your marks', says Alex. 'Set. Go!'

We're running.

In front of me, Olivia, Liza and Nasrin are sprinting fast, so I run fast too. Around the first bend I feel good. Liza, Nasrin and Olivia are still in front of me, but no one else has caught up. On the straight I gain on Liza and Nasrin and we run into the second bend together, with me just edging in front.

I hear a thump beside me. I look around, and see Nasrin sprawled over the track, her long black hair fanning around her. Liza has stopped running and is reaching down her hand.

I turn back and see Olivia still running. She's not stopping.

My hesitation has cost me time, but I'm not giving up now. I push myself harder. My legs hurt, but I ignore the pain. I am over halfway and I'm catching up to Olivia. As I go around the bend, I look back and across at Nasrin and Liza. They're both standing up again, and Nasrin seems fine.

We're on the home straight. I feel like heavy weights are attached to my thighs, dragging me down; my legs are aching and my chest is bursting. Olivia is only two metres in front. I get closer and closer. I am getting faster – even when it hurts, I can run faster.

We cross the finish line almost together, but not quite. Olivia has won, but I've come second again!

I look at the parents in the crowd, expecting to see them cheering for our exciting tight finish, but no one is looking at us. Everyone is still looking at the track where Liza and Nasrin are walking along the final straight. Nasrin has her arm over Liza's shoulder and Liza's arm is around Nasrin's waist. Alex is walking beside them. He didn't even see the end of my race.

Nasrin and Liza cross the finish line together. Nasrin bends down and hugs Liza. The parents are clapping their hands off. I clap too, even though I don't see what's so great about stacking it and having a walk.

After our last race we have the presentations. Principal Faye congratulates us for putting in a big effort. She says it's been the best school sports day ever, but she says that every year. She announces the points tally for the houses. Unfortunately, the You Yangs are still last and the Dandenongs are the winners.

They give out the Best Sportsperson awards for

each grade. When it comes to grade five, everyone knows the name Faye announces will be Olivia Indras because she nearly won everything.

Faye says, 'The winner of the grade five Best Sportsperson is someone who sacrificed her own race to help a fellow competitor. She is a new student at our school, and we are very lucky to welcome someone who so clearly embodies our values. It's Liza Gould!'

We are shocked. Matt and Kim are elbowing people and giving looks, so we clap. I look over at my dad and he and the other parents are cheering. Olivia is sitting next to me on the grass. She is clapping but she won't look up.

Liza walks up to the front, and Alex hands her the trophy. She shakes hands with Alex then Faye. She looks very serious, and I can't tell if she's pleased or not.

Olivia ties and unties her shoelaces.

Even from this distance the trophy is beautiful. It has a wooden base and a sparkly blue column with a statue of a gold athlete on the top.

When the presentations are over, Olivia and I stand up. 'Congratulations,' I say.

'What for?' says Olivia, like I've said something that doesn't make sense.

'The Dandenongs winning.'

Olivia shrugs. I follow her over to where her mum and my dad are chatting.

'Let's go, Mum,' says Olivia.

'Congratulations, Olivia,' says my dad. 'You did really well.'

'Thanks. We have to go, Mum,' says Olivia again.

'I'll come soon,' says Olivia's mother. But she rolls her eyes at Dad and says, 'I'd better get her home. It's been a big day.'

'Okay, see you soon. *Sampai jumpa*!' says Dad.

'*Sampai jumpa*,' says Olivia's mum. She's a high school Indonesian teacher so she's always very patient about Dad's Indonesian and the fact that he repeats himself.

Then Dad spots some other dad he knows. 'I'd better say hello to Damian.'

I'm left standing around with no one to talk to. Next to me, Liza is standing with her mum who is talking to Faye.

'What happened in the race?' I ask. I take a sip from my drink bottle.

'Nasrin tripped over,' says Liza.

'Did she trip you up too?'

'No, but it happened right in front of me.'

'You might have come third if you hadn't stopped.'

Liza shrugs. 'I guess we'll never know.' She pulls

the yellow ribbon out of her hair and ties it onto the base of her trophy. It looks even more beautiful.

'Don't you care about sport?' I ask, thinking she might be like Holly.

'I love sport!' says Liza. 'But I'm more into team sports like netball.'

'What position do you play?'

'I haven't been in an actual netball team yet. But I've watched a lot of games. Mum says I can join a team this season.'

'What position do you want to play?'

'Maybe goal keeper.'

I think you need to be tall for that, but I don't say anything because I don't want to be negative. Liza then tells me that she wants to play netball for Australia one day. That's her dream. Liza's not really so very different from Olivia and me after all.

Mum is late home after school sports day and I'm nearly finished eating by the time she gets to the table. She looks tired as she takes off her black jacket and hangs it on the back of the chair.

'You won't believe what the Board decided today!' she says to Dad.

'I'm sure I won't,' he says. 'But Vivian's had a big day too.'

'Sports day!' says Mum. 'How could I forget?'

'Just good luck,' says Noah.

Mum ignores Noah because that is the best policy. 'How did you go?'

'I got two second places.'

'What for?'

'The 100 metres and the 400 metres.' I take out my ribbons and show Mum.

'You don't win silver, you lose gold,' says Noah.

'You don't win anything if you don't try,' says Dad. He turns back to me. 'Will you be going to the interschool sports day, Viv?'

'Alex isn't sure,' I say. 'He doesn't know if just the winners will go or the people who came second too.'

'But the best part of the day was also in Vivian's last race,' says Dad. He tells them about Nasrin falling over and about how Liza helped her. He looks really excited, and I wonder if he'd be this excited if I won a race.

'It was like something out of a movie,' he says. 'I could almost hear the soundtrack swelling. Liza won Best Sportsperson, which was fantastic.'

'But Olivia was a bit disappointed,' I say. 'She won more blue ribbons than Liza.'

'Olivia needs to learn about good sportspersonship,' says Dad. 'There are other ways to be successful, not just by winning everything.'

'Olivia is good at all athletics,' I say.

'That's weird,' says Noah, from the kitchen sink where he's getting himself a drink of water.

'Why is it weird?' I ask.

'Indonesians aren't usually good at athletics.' He's about to sit back down with his water.

'Noah, could you please get water for everyone?' says Mum.

Noah rolls his eyes and trudges back to the sink as if it's a big deal.

'Olivia's not Indonesian,' I say.

'Yeah, I know she's Australian officially. But it's in your genes.' He puts a glass of water in front of me.

'That's not true,' I say. 'You're being racist.'

'I'm not! I'm being realistic. It's science.'

'Noah,' says Dad. 'You are not being helpful or kind. I also suspect that you're talking nonsense. A country's athletics results have more to do with sports funding than genetics.'

Noah shuts up.

I have a big drink because I need to rehydrate.

'Let's have ice-cream for dessert tonight to celebrate,' says Mum.

Mum and Dad talk about her Board meeting at work. Something about the budget needing to be redone to break even. Mum is really mad about it. Mum always says you can end up caring about boring stuff if you put your time and effort into it, but I can't imagine ever wanting to work in an office like she does.

After tea, I look up Indonesia's Olympic medal tallies on the computer, hoping to prove Noah wrong. Indonesia has never won a medal in athletics, but they are really good at badminton. They've won seven badminton gold medals and Australia doesn't have a single one.

Anyway, Olivia is winning everything and proving everyone wrong. Today I won four points for Team Olivian, but Olivia won seventeen. She will show them all.

I'm no closer to reaching my Olympic dream, but somehow, I still feel good about school sports day. Coming second is a lot better than coming second last, and I didn't need an ambulance. I'm starting to turn the corner.

5

REST

The day after school sports day, during art, I ask Liza if she wants to sit at our table at lunchtime. She says she might come over to say hello.

'What did you do that for?' asks Olivia when we go to the paste station to get more paste.

'Do what?'

'Ask Liza to sit with us.'

'She's nice.'

'We've got nothing in common.'

Olivia is making assumptions about Liza because she wears glasses and once wore a dress to school.

'That's not true,' I say. 'She doesn't look sporty, but she actually wants to play netball for Australia.'

'It's not even an Olympic sport.'

‘That’s not Liza’s fault.’

Olivia just rolls her eyes.

Liza does come and sit with us at lunchtime. Liza and I talk about her old school. It sounds quite a lot like Wallaby Flat Primary except they only had one netball court and we have two.

While we’re eating Alex walks past on yard duty. He’s not wearing his high-visibility vest. I hope Faye doesn’t see or he will be in trouble again.

‘I just need to ask Alex something,’ I say to the others. Maybe Olivia will talk to Liza while I’m gone, but I won’t get my hopes up.

I hurry over. ‘Um, Alex,’ I say.

‘Yes, Vivian?’ Alex says, without looking at me because he’s watching some boys on the monkey bars.

‘You know the interschool sports day?’

‘Yes, I do know it.’

‘Well, do you know yet who gets to go? Is it just the people who came first on school sports day?’

‘Oh yeah. I asked about that. Apparently, we can only have one boy and one girl for each event.’

‘Even if two girls were the fastest?’

‘That’s right.’

‘So I won’t be going?’

‘No, sorry, mate,’ he says, still not looking at me.

'Maybe next year.' Then Alex strides away from me to the play equipment. 'Do not jump from there, Daniel!' he shouts.

Sometimes I wonder if Alex will ever see my potential.

I go back to the table and tell Olivia and Liza I won't be going to interschool sports day. Everyone agrees that it's really unfair. If two girls are the fastest, two girls should go.

Olivia says she wishes she'd let me win the 400 metres. I know she would never let me win, but it's nice of her to say.

Liza says that's the good thing about netball – the teams have at least seven people, so there's more chance of getting a place on the team.

They are both trying to cheer me up, but it doesn't really work.

Olivia suggests we play handball. Liza is really good, and I have to work very hard, so at least that takes my mind off my problems.

Olivia and Liza both go for the ball at the same time and crash into each other. Liza's glasses go flying off. They don't break, and I think it was an accident, so that's okay.

On Saturday, Mum and I go for a long walk. Mum has a rule that she never works on the weekend, so I make her leave her phone at home so she won't get distracted and accidentally reply to a work email.

It's a sunny day and we head away from the main road, down our dirt road to the river. I get bored walking. I jog on ahead and then jog back to Mum.

'I thought we were supposed to be walking together?' says Mum.

'You're too slow,' I say.

When we get to the river, we sit on a rock to eat our muffins. I tell Mum about how Liza is sitting with our group now and how Olivia is being weird.

'It sounds like Olivia is a bit jealous,' says Mum.

'Why?'

'Because you're making friends with other people. She's used to having the Olivians to herself.'

I'm not sure about that. 'I think she might be jealous about the award at sports day.'

'Maybe that too,' says Mum.

'Olivia doesn't need to be worried. Liza doesn't even want to go to the Olympics. She wants to be a professional netballer.'

'Feelings don't always make a lot of sense.'

'And at least Olivia gets to go to the interschool sports day,' I say. 'She is actually the lucky one.'

I finish my muffin and Mum and I stand up and start walking home. Mum gets puffed out halfway up the first hill and has to stop for a rest. She won't see any improvement in her fitness if she stops every time it gets difficult. When the going gets tough, the tough get going. 'You need to push through!' I say.

'I need a break!'

'No, come on, you can do it!' I hope I'm inspiring her. I bounce up and down on the spot and say, 'Come on, if we jog we'll get to the top of the hill faster!'

Mum jogs very slowly. It's not a proper jog, but at least she's moving again. I walk fast beside her and try to remember motivational exercise quotes. 'The pain you feel today is the strength you'll have tomorrow,' I say.

Mum rolls her eyes.

'It never gets easier; you just get better.'

Mum makes a weird noise so I don't think she liked that one.

I try again. 'You earn your body.'

Mum stops. We are at the top of the hill.

'Great work! You made it!' I say.

Mum is panting. 'I … don't … ever … want to hear that from you … again,' she says.

'What?'

'You don't earn your body. It's—' Mum leans over with her hands on her thighs. Then she falls to her knees and tips forward flat on her face on the dirt road.

'Mum! Mum!' I shout. She's lying on her stomach with her head to one side. Her eyes are closed.

Oh no. Mum.

I don't know what to do. Should I check her pulse? Is she breathing? Should I run for help?

Mum opens her eyes. 'What happened?' she says.

'I think you fainted.' I sound shaky because I'm so relieved.

'I'm so sorry,' she says. 'That was so weird.'

'It's okay. Can you get up now?'

'Yes, yes, of course.'

I hold her arm and she leans on me to stand up. She is shaking. Mum cut her forehead and her arm when she fell. Blood is trickling down her face and her elbow. I help her to the side of the road, where she sits on a tree stump.

'I'll get Dad.'

'No, I just need to rest for a bit.'

'We need Dad.'

Mum closes her eyes and nods.

I run.

It's at least three kilometres back to the house. I should pace myself, but all I can think about is Mum lying on the ground. What if she faints again? She doesn't have her phone with her. Hardly anyone drives down that road. She'll be all alone.

I speed up, breathing hard. What if she dies? My legs burn but I keep running because what does it matter if my legs hurt compared to Mum dying. Coming up to the driveway, I sprint. Dad is out at the chooks.

'Dad!' I yell. 'Mum's sick!'

'What?' he says, looking confused.

'There's something wrong with Mum!' I shout.

'Where is she?'

'Near the river hill. I think she fainted.'

'Get in the car.' Dad sounds like he's angry at me, but I think it's only because he's worried.

The drive seems to take longer than the run did.

'Go faster!' I tell Dad.

'I'm driving as fast as I safely can,' says Dad. 'There's no point us having an accident.'

Finally, we pull up beside Mum. She's still sitting on the stump, and she looks much better, not grey and wobbly like before.

'Are you okay?' asks Dad as we hurry out of the car.

'Yes, I'm fine. I just overdid it a bit. Vivian was a little too motivating.'

Dad opens the passenger door for Mum and

helps her in. Mum fishes the first-aid kit out of the glove box and finds a piece of white cloth to hold against the cut on her forehead.

'I think we should go to Emergency,' says Dad.

'God no!' says Mum. 'I'm not sitting around there all day.'

'What about your head?' asks Dad.

'The bleeding's stopped already,' says Mum. 'It's not very deep. Head wounds always bleed a lot.'

'Do they?' I ask.

'That's what they say on TV,' says Mum.

'You'll have to go to the GP on Monday then,' says Dad.

Mum doesn't reply, so Dad says, 'Seriously. You can't ignore this.'

'What will a doctor say to me?'

'I don't know – I'm a graphic designer. That's the point.'

'There's nothing wrong with me.'

'Well, it would be good to hear that from a medical professional not a business analyst,' Dad says, sounding a bit angry again. '*I* would like some reassurance, even if you don't.'

'You should go, Mum,' I say. 'You didn't look very good.'

'Vivian was great!' says Mum. 'Maybe you'll be a doctor, Viv?' She turns around and smiles at me.

The blood has soaked through the cloth on her forehead.

I don't want to be a doctor and Mum knows that.

On Monday morning, Olivia and I meet at the bottom of the hill. 'Did you do any training on the weekend?' I ask.

'A bit.' She doesn't go into details, which is unusual for her. Suddenly she says, 'Do you think Liza is going to sit with us now?'

'I don't know. Maybe.'

'Why doesn't she sit with Holly and those girls?'

'Liza's not into horses. You know what that lot are like.'

'I guess so.'

'Do you mind if she sits with us?' I ask.

'No.' She rolls her eyes like it was a weird question to ask.

But I know she does mind. When Holly tried to join our group, it was horrible. Olivia actually made a sign that said, 'Reserved for the Olivians', and stuck it to the table. I had to pretend it was a joke, but I think Holly felt bad.

Luckily, Holly only wanted to sit with us because everyone else in her group got a pony and she felt left out. Then it turned out that Nasrin didn't really have a pony, she just took a photo with one in a paddock. So Holly went back to her old group. It was a relief, to be honest. Not because I don't like Holly, but because it made Olivia so grumpy.

Olivia's mum once told my mum that Olivia takes a while to warm up to people. Her mum told my mum that every time they go to visit their family in Jakarta it takes Olivia two weeks to start talking to her cousins. And then it's time to come home again. I'm not supposed to know about that, but I overheard Mum tell Dad.

I hope Olivia will warm up to Liza soon. Even though Olivia is a great friend and the only person who really understands me, I like talking to other people too.

We have assembly first thing because it's Monday. Principal Faye says she has an exciting announcement. I hope it won't be about the Tidy Schools Competition. We did that last year, and the idea of a competition sounded great, until it turned out to be just picking up rubbish. Our school came third in the Bendigo region and we won a worm farm.

Faye says, 'Next week we will be holding the cross country competition for grades four to six. As you know, last year the cross country was cancelled due to … circumstances.'

On the day of the cross country last year our old PE teacher, Brendan, sat on the roof for three hours and refused to come down. Eventually the fire brigade came, and Brendan went home and never came back to school. I heard he works at the swimming pool now, which I hope he likes more than being a teacher. Anyway, that's why we missed the race last year.

'The race will be three kilometres, and *everyone* is expected to participate,' Faye says. 'Your teachers will hand out permission forms this afternoon.'

Olivia nudges me and whispers, 'Team Olivian is going to smash it!'

After the school sports day I've realised that there isn't really any such thing as Team Olivian. Olivia and I both can't win.

At recess Liza sits with us and Olivia doesn't seem to mind because she's too excited about the cross country. Olivia says she's not good at long distance because she's a sprinter, but it will be useful cardio training for the interschool sports day. I'm worried about the distance. I ran three kilometres on the weekend, but that was an actual emergency.

Liza is not very excited about the cross country because it's not netball, but she says it's always nice to get out and about.

*

After school Mum picks me up for a change. We go into town for her doctor's appointment. I'm glad she's being checked out, for reassurance. Mum has a big bandaid on her forehead. She's worried that people are staring at it. They probably are because it's really obvious.

When the doctor calls Mum, I stay in the waiting room to give her privacy. I find a recent copy of *Athletics World* in the magazine pile. I read 'The 20 Best Tips for Training in Winter'. I'm very interested in this because the weather is getting colder. One of the tips is to go to bed early and make sure you get enough sleep.

The next article is about whether too much sleep could undermine a training plan.

I'm confused about whether I sleep the right amount. I will ask Olivia about it because she always has good advice.

Mum comes out of the doctor's office and goes to the reception desk to pay.

Then we have to go to yet another waiting room because Mum needs blood tests so they can rule things out. Mum takes a number and we sit down. There are no magazines in this room.

'How much sleep do you get?' I ask Mum.

'I don't know. Not enough.'

'How many hours? On average?'

‘I don’t know. Six?’

‘Six! You need at least seven according to *Athletics World*.’

‘Well, I’m not an athlete, remember? And I sleep in on Sundays.’

It seems Mum’s training schedule won’t be undermined by her having too much sleep. Not that she has a training schedule, if we’re honest.

The nurse comes out and says, ‘Number twenty-four.’

Mum follows her into the blood-taking room. I’m glad it’s Mum and not me. I hate needles. Last year we had our flu vaccinations at school. Holly went first, and when she came out, she told us she felt the needle touch the bone in her arm. I got so nervous waiting for my turn that I fainted. Daniel teased me for ages and said everyone could see my undies when I was unconscious, even though Olivia said that definitely wasn’t true and it doesn’t even matter because we were all girls in the room. After I fainted, I went to the sick bay to lie down and they gave me the vaccination there. It didn’t even hurt, and the needle definitely didn’t touch the bone. I must have a high pain threshold compared to Holly. Dad picked me up and I got to go home early, so the joke was on Daniel, really.

Mum looks fine when she comes out of the room.

'Did you faint?' I ask.

'Of course not,' says Mum.

Her phone rings on the way to the car and Mum answers, 'Hi, darl,' so I know she's talking to Dad. 'Just like I thought, she had no idea. I had a blood test, but that won't show anything. And I'm supposed to have an ECG. I don't have time for this at the moment. Anyway, we're at the car, we'll see you soon.'

Mum puts her phone in the bag. 'Your father is such a worrier!' she says.

That's true. He always thinks we're going to get salmonella poisoning from chicken, so he cooks it for too long and it goes tough.

Back at home I have time for a walk before tea. To prepare for the school cross country I run through the paddocks. It's fun swishing through the grass. I climb through a fence and run across the next paddock. I'm sure the Petersons won't mind.

When I get home my socks are full of grass seeds. I didn't notice them prickling when I was running. While I'm sitting on the steps picking the grass seeds out, Noah and Dad arrive home from concert band practice.

‘Hello, Viv,’ says Dad, making his way past me to the back door.

‘You stink!’ says Noah.

‘That’s the smell of effort, Noah,’ says Dad.

‘It’s the smell of B.O.’

The wooden steps shake under me as Noah stomps up into the house. He bangs the door, angrily, behind him.

‘Don’t worry about him,’ says Dad. ‘It’s not about you. I just told him he has to play footy this year or he can’t go on music camp.’

‘But Noah loves music camp.’

‘It’s for his own good,’ says Dad.

6

CROSS COUNTRY

On the day of the school cross country we get ready at lunchtime. Olivia takes Liza and me through some stretches.

When the end-of-lunchtime song plays, we walk to the oval where the race will start.

Olivia says to me, 'What's our race plan, Olivian?'

'What do you mean? I was just going to run.'

'You can't just run. This isn't a sprint. You need to pace yourself.'

I don't know as much about running as Olivia. Up until school sports day I'd been concentrating on long jump.

Olivia sighs, but she comes up with a plan. 'I tell you what – we'll both pace each other out for the first half and then see who can kick from there.'

'Okay.' I don't understand what she's talking about, but I'll try to run with her and see what happens.

Only grades four, five and six will do the school cross country because the other grades are too little. The preps would wander about and get lost and then the cross country would be cancelled forever.

It's my first ever cross country race. We didn't get to do it last year because Brendan, the old PE teacher, was sitting on the roof.

Alex gets everyone to be quiet and then explains where we'll run.

We will go across the grass to the back gate of the school, turn left, then run along the road for 200 metres until we get to the turn-off leading down to the creek. We'll run down the little hill and onto the creek path, and run one kilometre until we see Kim. Then we'll turn around at the witch's hat and come back the same way. Teachers will stand along the course to make sure no one gets lost. Everyone is expected to participate and try their hardest.

My heart is beating faster, the back of my neck is sweating, and we're not even running yet.

'Can we get on with it?' says Daniel. He's bouncing up and down, which I think is a waste of energy.

'Daniel, you'll be disqualified if you don't learn some patience,' says Faye.

I am very confused about whether they want everyone to participate or not.

'Okay then, everybody!' Alex says. 'Get behind the start line.'

We bunch up together behind the line Alex has drawn in the dirt next to the oval. Olivia grabs my hand and pulls me towards the front. 'We should have a priority start,' she says to me. Then she nudges a grade four boy and says, 'Make room for the Olivians. Move!'

We are now right at the front in the middle. My stomach is churning, like I need to go to the toilet, but I have missed my chance.

Alex says, 'On your marks. Go!'

We set off across the oval. Some of the little grade four kids sprint, but when we get to the native grass area they are already tired and slowing down. Olivia and I run past them. Someone else is running on my left. I look and see Sam.

My legs feel weak and shaky, but I think that's because I'm nervous. I push through it.

The native grass area is on a little slope towards the school's back gate and I accelerate down it. Beside me, Olivia says, 'We should pace ourselves.'

Sam, Olivia and I run through the gateway together and on to the road.

It's easier to run on the hard bitumen. Matt is standing by the side of the road wearing a fluorescent yellow vest. A sign next to him reads, 'Warning: Runners on Road', but there aren't any cars around.

As we run past, Matt shouts, 'Good work Olivians and Sam! Keep it up! Turn left down to the creek.'

We take the little turn-off and run down the hill towards the creek path. I let the hill pull me down, making me sprint.

Sam, Olivia and I are still in the lead. The creek path twists and turns so we can't see the turn-around point ahead.

'We're … supposed to … pace ourselves,' Olivia says.

If I slow down now Sam will get ahead.

It's a long way to the finish, so I won't think about that. I only think about making it past the next bend. Then the next one. Olivia drops back behind Sam and me.

Now I can see Kim up ahead. 'We're nearly halfway!' I yell to Olivia behind me.

Kim claps and waves. 'Great work, Vivian!' she says. 'Go right around the witch's hat!'

I run past her, and pivot around the orange cone. Sam and Olivia run towards me coming up to the halfway point. I could wait for Olivia but she's slowed down a lot and I don't need to.

I'm more than halfway through the race. Every step gets me closer to the finish.

I pass kids coming in the opposite direction who are still running towards the turn-around point. I come up to Liza and she says, 'You're winning! Keep it up!'

Behind Liza is Calvin. His face is red, and I can hear his breathing from 50 metres away. I'm worried he might collapse. 'Are you alright?' I say as I pass him, and he says, 'Yes!'

I'm relieved that I don't have to worry about him for good sportspersonship.

Holly is right at the back. She is walking with a group of grade fours and doesn't look puffed, so I don't think she's been trying her hardest. At least she's participating.

When I reach the hill up to the road my legs hurt, but I push myself not to slow down. I think about Chloe Esposito and how powerful she looked running to the finish line.

Back on the bitumen, Matt is still there to stop the traffic and there still isn't any traffic. 'Go Vivian,' he says. 'Run, run, run!'

I'm winning now but Olivia was right – I should have paced myself. I'm dizzy from going up the hill and the muscles in my thighs are on fire. I can't do it. I'm going to stop. I want to stop.

I get to the gate and go through. I run through the native grasses. I remember running through the paddock near home. A grass seed in my sock is prickling my ankle.

A lot of little kids are waiting at the finish line on the other side of the oval. The other grades in the school have come out to watch us finish. It would be so embarrassing to stop with everyone watching. I count my strides in my head and when I reach twenty the finish line is only 50 metres in front of me. Only a few more seconds to go.

I cross the line. It's over.

I bend over, resting my hands on my knees. The race is done and I didn't slow down!

I turn expecting see Olivia and Sam crossing the line just after me. But I can't see them.

Alex comes over and says, 'Good running, Vivian!'

'Where are the others?' I ask while trying to catch my breath.

'You dropped them all,' says Alex. 'They're still coming.'

I wait, staring across the oval. When another

runner appears, it's not Sam or Olivia like I expected. It's a grade four kid, Madeline. I clap as she crosses the finish line.

Sam is next, and after him, lots more people finish. A big group comes through together and they sprint to the finish when they clearly weren't running that fast the whole time.

I'm worried about Olivia. Maybe her Achilles injury has flared up again.

Finally, Liza and Olivia appear in the native grasses. They're jogging beside each other, and they cross the oval together and don't race each other at the end. I look at the timing clock and see that they've finished almost seven minutes after me.

Liza comes straight over. 'Did you win?' she asks as she tries to get her breath back.

'Yeah. Is Olivia okay?'

'I think so.'

Olivia sits by herself on the grass.

Calvin is coming across the oval now. He looks even more puffed out than when I saw him on the road. He crosses the line, raises his hands in the air and yells, 'Champion! Now, where's my gold medal?'

It's pretty funny and everyone claps for him.

Holly walks across the line followed by the teachers, so she must be the last kid.

I get a blue ribbon. My first blue ribbon ever. The gold letters say, 'Winner, 1st Prize'. Liza and Olivia get purple ribbons.

When Alex gives me the ribbon, he tells me that I've qualified for the district cross country.

'Is that the same as the interschool sports day?' I ask.

'No, it's the week after.'

I don't care because the district cross country sounds even better than the interschool sports day because it's for the whole district.

Olivia and Liza are sitting together on the grass and I go over to show them my ribbon.

'More points for Team Olivian!' I say.

Olivia smiles, but it doesn't last long.

'What's Team Olivian anyway?' asks Liza.

'That's what we call ourselves,' I explain.

'It's a thing we made up ages ago,' says Olivia. 'I think it's getting a bit old now.'

At tea time I tell Mum and Dad that I won the school cross country and that I've qualified for the district cross country. I give them a blow-by-blow description of the race so it's like they were there.

'When I got to the bitumen, I didn't think I could keep running. I thought the race would never end,' I say.

'It probably felt a lot like this story,' says Noah.

Noah has to apologise or leave the table. He apologises.

Noah shouldn't be so negative. Susie Maroney says having a positive attitude is what got her through the tough times, like when she got seasick and kept spewing while she swam across the English Channel. No wonder Noah never achieves anything. Also, being negative is bad for your health because it increases toxins.

I still can't believe I beat Olivia in a race. She beat me in *six events* at the school sports day. People might say I had no chance, like my dad racing against Usain Bolt. But I didn't give up, and in the end, I won.

Mum makes Noah and me do the dishes after tea. I stack the dishwasher while Noah washes the big pots because Mum says he's good at it.

I try to talk to Noah about his day.

'What did you do at lunchtime?' I ask.

'Nothing.'

'What do you mean, *nothing*?'

'I mean, I didn't do anything.'

'Who'd you sit with?'

'Tom.'

'Do you talk about stuff?'

'Sometimes. Not much.'

'Do you play games like handball?'

'No.' He shakes his head and laughs. 'People don't play games at high school. Except in PE when they make you.'

'That sounds so boring. I'm going to play games when I'm at high school.'

'No, you won't.'

I don't bother arguing with him because that's the best policy, but I know I will *never* sit around doing nothing when I could be playing handball or sardines or pretending to be an emergency service worker. Olivia and Liza will never be like that either.

7
PREPARATION

The next morning, I arrive at the bottom of the hill early. I can't wait to talk to Olivia about my training plan.

She's not there yet, so I sit on the grass and do stretches while I wait.

It's not like Olivia to be late because her parents are high school teachers and they have to get to work before nine. I wait for ten minutes, and then I walk to school by myself. Maybe Olivia is sick even though she has a great immune system.

I hurry up the hill, but it's awkward jogging with my backpack. I don't want to be late because Matt hates that. I can hear the song playing, which means the bell will ring soon. The song is about feeling happy and clapping and a roof. It doesn't make sense. I get to our classroom just as the song stops and the bell rings.

I see Olivia and Liza walking up the ramp together. Liza sees me and smiles and waves, but Olivia must be in a hurry because she doesn't turn around.

Maybe Olivia thought I wasn't coming to school this morning, so she didn't wait for me? Maybe her Achilles tendon is playing up again and she couldn't walk up the hill? Maybe her mum had to talk to Matt before school?

I follow Liza and Olivia up the ramp and put my bag away in my locker. I take out my pencil case, which Olivia gave me for my birthday. It's made completely out of zippers. It looks really cool but it's hard to keep closed and I'm always losing pens.

At my desk, I sit down, and say, 'Hi!' to Olivia, thinking it's weird that she hasn't noticed me yet.

'Class is starting,' she replies, still facing the front.

Matt explains what we'll be doing today. Apparently, we have a lot to get through and we've missed a lot of learning time, what with 'one thing and another'. I think he means sport.

We do history and society first. Matt tells us that because it's an Olympic year we will be studying the Olympics.

Olivia gasps. She usually hates history and society, but this is different.

'But we won't be studying sport,' says Matt.

'Damn,' mutters Olivia.

'We'll be studying the politics and history of the Olympics.'

Matt starts at the very beginning of the Olympic Games, which means the ones they used to have in Athens. They started nearly 3000 years ago and were held every four years for hundreds of years. At first, the Olympics was just one running race, but later they held discus, javelin and long jump events as well.

Then the Olympics in Greece had a break for around 1500 years until people decided to start the Olympics again in Athens in 1896. The next one was in Paris in 1900, but it wasn't very good. Since then, there's been a summer Olympic Games every four years, except during the world wars. The Winter Olympics were first held in 1924 and the Paralympics in 1960.

The Olympic Games are different from other sporting events because they're meant to represent values like equality, living a good life, and doing your best. The Olympics aren't just about winning medals and being famous. It's about improving humanity. I can't wait to be there.

Matt tells us that we are going to do Olympic debating. We will be in teams of three and we don't get to pick our own teams. Matt draws names out of a hat.

I end up with Liza and Calvin on my team. We are Team Spain. Olivia is in a team with Sam and Holly. They are Team USA.

Matt writes the four debating topics on the board:

That the Olympic Games should be cancelled
That the minimum age for Olympic competitors be raised to 18 years
That video games should be included as an Olympic sport
That we should stop drug testing Olympic athletes

All the topics are ridiculous. None of them are true.

Next, Matt writes teams next to the topics. My team, Team Spain, gets 'That the Olympic Games should be cancelled'. Then Matt says that Team Spain will be arguing in the *negative*. So we'll be saying that the Olympic Games *shouldn't* be cancelled. It is a big relief.

We're going to be debating against Team USA, Olivia's team. I feel sorry for them. Matt says that the point of debating is to make a good argument, even if you don't believe it, but it would be horrible to argue for something ridiculous like cancelling the Olympics.

Matt gives us time to work in our groups. Calvin, Liza and I make a list of reasons why the Olympics shouldn't be cancelled. I didn't think Calvin would be good at it because he doesn't even want to go to the Olympics, but he comes up with good ideas and tells us about infrastructure.

REASONS WHY THE OLYMPIC GAMES SHOULD NOT BE CANCELLED:
Unite the world
Good for the economy
Inspiration
Careers for athletes
Infrastructure
Health

At recess, Olivia wants to have a skipping competition. It turns out that Olivia can skip without stopping for longer than Liza or me. She seems a bit more cheerful after that.

The next day, for the second day in a row, Olivia isn't waiting for me at the bottom of the hill. So Mum takes me straight to school. When I get to class, Olivia and Liza are at our table, talking about injuries. Liza once broke her leg, and Olivia can relate to that because in grade one she fell off the monkey bars and broke her wrist.

We have sport with Alex first. For our warm-up he tells us to run around the oval. We jog in a big group at first, but then Sam sprints to the front and Olivia follows him because she can't resist a race, even though it's only supposed to be a warm-up. I stay back with Liza.

Next, Alex tells us to do a faster lap. This time I run with Sam and Olivia. After we run past the second goalpost, I pick up speed again, but so do Sam and Olivia. The three of us finish in a dead heat.

'Nice. You're keeping each other honest,' says Alex.

I get my breath back while the rest of the class finishes.

'Now, Vivian, I'd like you to do a lap by yourself.'

'Why?'

'Off you go.'

I jog around the boundary line again.

'Pick it up, Vivian!' yells Alex. I run a bit faster. I pass the first set of goalposts, and when I turn, I see the whole class looking at me. I hope I don't trip and fall flat on my face in front of everyone. I hate it when that happens.

I try to ignore the class, and just look straight ahead and finish the lap as fast as I can.

When I'm finished Alex says, 'Thanks for that, Vivian.'

Alex hands out the footballs and we pair up to practise handballing.

Liza and Olivia are in a pair again. I know I wanted Olivia to be friends with Liza, and I am happy for them, but I wish I wasn't left on my own.

I go in a pair with Holly.

'What was Alex saying when I was running?' I ask her.

'He was telling us about your technique.'

'What technique?'

'He was going on about how you get your knees up high, and how your feet strike the ground, and how your knees and arms are in a straight line. Stuff like that.'

'Oh. Was he saying it's bad?' I ask.

'No, no. He thinks you're really good.'

I feel excited and pleased because this is what I wanted – for Alex to see I have potential. But I'm also nervous because now he has expectations, and I don't want to let him down.

Someone laughs really loudly and I look over and see Olivia and Liza are having a great time. It's quite distracting for the rest of the class. I think Alex should say something to them, but he doesn't.

At the end of morning sport our class walks back to the portable. I walk up beside Olivia and say, 'That was fun.'

'Oh my god, Vivian!' she says.

'What?'

'You stink.'

Everyone hears her, and some people laugh.

'You really need to get some deodorant.'

My face feels hot. I think I probably look like a tomato in a wig, like Noah said. I keep my face down and hope Olivia doesn't say anything else.

We get to the portable, and I ask Matt if I can go to the toilet straight away.

The girls' toilet block is empty. I rip off a piece of hand towel from the roll and wet it to wipe under my arms. I get spots of water on my T-shirt, so I stand under the hand-dryer. The warm air blows on my face. I don't want to sweat more, so I turn off the dryer. I sniff under my arms. I don't think I smell, but I read somewhere that you can't smell yourself.

When I get back to the portable Matt asks, 'Are you okay, Vivian?'

'Yes.'

I walk to my seat with my head down and don't look at anyone. Olivia says hello when I sit down, but I don't say anything back because I think I might cry.

I don't put my hand up to answer questions for the rest of the day, just to be on the safe side.

That night I stand at the kitchen bench watching Mum chop the carrots for tea.

'If you've got nothing to do, Vivian, you can start on the potatoes.'

I get five potatoes out of the cupboard. I take them to the sink and peel them. 'Mum,' I say.

'Vivian,' Mum says.

'Well, I was just wondering …'

'Yes, what were you wondering?'

Mum sounds impatient, so I try to get to the point. 'You know deodorant?'

'I do know it, yes.'

'Well, could you get me some?'

Mum stops chopping. 'Why do you want that?'

'Because I'm doing more running, and I think I need it.'

'Girls your age don't need deodorant. You don't need it until you're a teenager.'

'But I don't want to smell.'

'You don't smell. It's marketing to suck you in. They want you to get hooked on their products while you're young. Don't fall for it, Viv.' Mum waves a carrot dismissively and that's the end of the conversation.

I hand Mum the peeled potatoes then I go to my room. I look out my window and see Noah in the backyard. He's kicking the footy against the shed wall and catching it when it bounces back. I'm worried he'll break a window, but at least he looks like he's having fun.

I sit down on my bed. I want to win, but I don't want to smell bad. I remember Michael, who left our school in grade two. He definitely smelled bad, kind of like a mixture of fish and wee, and no one wanted to play with him. Everyone called him 'Stinky Minky'. I wonder if I've been smelling for ages and no one except Olivia would tell me.

The next day is Saturday and I go into town with Mum. At the supermarket Mum asks me to get shampoo and conditioner so I go to the personal hygiene products aisle. I choose the brand we always get. I notice the deodorants on the opposite shelf. They have the kind Olivia has. Sometimes she lets me have a spray, but I can't rely on that.

I'm wearing my hoodie with the front pockets. I'm the only person in the personal hygiene products aisle. I could take a deodorant. That would solve all my problems.

I take the shampoo and conditioner to put in Mum's trolley.

Mum wants to have morning tea at the café after the supermarket. I want to go straight home.

'You can have a chocolate croissant,' says Mum.

'They're not good for you,' I say.

'You're no fun,' says Mum.

We go to the café anyway because I get no say in our family. I have a cold-pressed juice and Mum has a coffee and a pastry.

When I get home, I go straight to my room, but there's a knock on the door. I assume Mum has come to tell me to help unpack the shopping.

Mum says, 'Here you go,' and hands me a deodorant.

'Thanks.' I'm so surprised. She hardly ever changes her mind about anything.

'Now, come and help me with the shopping.'

So some things never change.

In the kitchen, I load vegetables into the crisper. At the bottom of a shopping bag I find frozen chips. That's not a healthy choice. When Mum's not looking, I put the packet of chips in the bin then cover it over with other rubbish. It's for our own good.

I tell Mum I'm going for a run.

'Not a walk?' she asks.

'No, I'm training for the district cross country.'

I set off towards the river. And I think about how Olivia seems mad at me.

I thought Mum was right and she was jealous of Liza joining our group. But now Olivia seems okay with Liza, and it's me she doesn't like. Why else would she embarrass me in front of the whole class?

I run almost to the river before I turn around. It's boring running by myself compared to being in a race, so I imagine someone is running just in front of me. Someone like Sam. I wouldn't want him to beat me.

8

DISTRICTS

Olivia is away at interschool sports day on Wednesday, so it's just me and Liza at the table for lunch. We are trying to throw mandarin pips into Liza's lunch box at the end of the table.

'She'll definitely win the sprints,' I say. I throw a pip and it lands in the middle of the lunch box, but then bounces out.

'Unlucky,' says Liza. 'The high jump might be more difficult for Olivia.' Liza throws a pip, but completely misses and it sails over the lunch box.

'I think she'll win them all,' I say.

'I'm not saying that she won't,' Liza says. 'I just think high jump might be trickier because it's not her strongest event. Sam did beat her at school sports day.'

'Let's not be negative.'

'I'm not. I'm just saying, you guys always think winning is everything.' Liza throws another pip and this time manages to hit the side of the lunch box.

Winning isn't everything – but it is pretty important if you want to be an elite athlete. Liza needs to learn that if she wants to play netball for Australia. I throw my last pip and it lands in the box. I am five for five, if you count the one that bounced out, which I do.

At the end of the day, just as the final bell rings, the minibus arrives back from the interschool sports day. We rush out of the portable to meet it.

As soon as I see Olivia, I know it's not good news. She's looking at the ground and her shoulders are slumped.

Olivia barely glances up when we get to her.

'What happened?' I ask.

'Not much.'

'Did you get any ribbons?'

'Just this one.' She holds up a green ribbon. Green is for third.

'Which event?' I ask.

'One hundred metres.'

'Who beat you?'

'I don't know. A couple of girls from another school.'

'What about the other events?' asks Liza.

Olivia shrugs again.

I know how she feels. I was the same after the school swimming carnival, and my first soccer game, and gymnastics.

'Do you want to come over this afternoon?' Olivia asks me.

'Yeah, sure,' I say. But then I remember. 'Actually, I'm supposed to be going to Liza's.'

'That's okay,' says Liza. 'We can do it another day. Or Olivia could come over too.'

'Forget it,' says Olivia, and she turns and walks off.

'No, I can come!' I call after her. But she's getting in her mum's car so I don't think she heard me.

At Liza's house we have goji berries and juice for afternoon tea. I'm not allowed to drink juice at home even though fruit is good for you, because Dad says juice is full of so much sugar that you may as well drink Coke. But Liza's mum makes us a special juice with kale and carrots. It looks disgusting, but it tastes nice because she adds honey and pineapple.

We go to the lounge room to watch *Salute*, which is about a race at the Mexico Olympics.

Tommie Smith and John Carlos from the USA came first and third in the 200 metres men's final, and when they stood on the dais to get their medals, they both did a black power salute because they wanted people to know about inequality in America. Peter Norman, the Australian who came second, wore a pin because he agreed with them about equality.

They all got in big trouble because the Olympics shouldn't be political. People said the salute was against the Olympic spirit, but I don't think that's true. The Olympics should be about everyone being equal, so their protest was in the Olympic spirit.

I am more convinced than ever that the Olympics should not be cancelled because athletes can raise attention to very important issues, even if they're not supposed to.

'I'm so glad people aren't racist anymore,' says Liza.

'I think they still are sometimes,' I say.

'Really?'

'Yeah, people say some bad things to Olivia's family.'

'That's terrible. Like what?'

Liza wants to hear about the bad things, as though it will be really interesting, but I don't want to repeat what the men yelled out from the car at Olivia's birthday picnic. 'I can't remember,' I say.

We go back to the kitchen. 'Olivia seemed pretty upset today,' Liza says.

'Yeah. I think she was disappointed.'

'But she shouldn't take it out on everyone else.'

I understand how Olivia feels, though. I was the same after the swimming carnival when I realised I couldn't be an Olympic swimmer, triathlete, water polo player or synchronised swimmer. Mum and Dad were worried I was grumpy because I hit my head in the pool, but that wasn't it. I was just disappointed and frustrated. But then Olivia and I came up with a new plan and it was okay.

Team Olivian has to stick together at times like these.

Liza shows me her room. She has a poster of a netball player on her wall. I ask who it is. Liza explains that Sharni Layton was a great netball defender who joined the AFL women's league. She went from one non-Olympic sport to another, which I find hard to understand, but I know some people have different priorities.

'Do you want to see my gemstone collection?' asks Liza.

'Sure,' I say. I'm just being polite, but when Liza

gets out the box from her wardrobe and shows me, it's actually more interesting than I thought. Each rock is different, and the colours and patterns are beautiful.

Liza tells me that some of the stones have healing powers. If she's sick, Liza sleeps with a blue rock under her pillow, and when she wakes up, she always feels better. I think Liza probably just feels better after a sleep, but I don't say that.

Liza's mum drops me home and I check on tea, but Dad is still cooking. I have time for a quick training run.

I stop running once because I feel like I might throw up, but it passes. I'm not sure goji berries are as good for you as people say, or maybe you're not supposed to eat that many.

The next day Olivia is waiting for me at the bottom of the hill.

'Stop the car!' I yell at Mum.

Mum slams on the breaks. 'What's wrong?'

'Nothing. I just want to get out here.'

'Jesus, Vivian! Don't do that to me. You'll give me a heart attack.'

'Sorry. See you tonight.'

When I get out of the car Olivia says, 'Sorry about yesterday.'

'That's okay.'

'What was Liza's house like?' Olivia asks.

'Good. I ate too many goji berries, though.'

I nearly tell Olivia about the good documentary we watched, but I don't want to give away hints about our debate arguments.

Olivia sniffs. I step a little further away from her.

'Are you wearing Waterberry deodorant?'

'Yeah.'

'It's really nice.'

We walk up the hill. 'I'm so sore,' says Olivia.

'Six events is a lot. You might need to focus on one or two events.'

'Maybe.'

'You might need to refresh your training program as well. How much sleep have you been getting?'

'I don't know. Enough.' Olivia pauses. 'I don't want to be an Olympic sprinter anymore,' she says. 'I'm going to be a scientist.'

'What?'

'I'm going to be a sports scientist.'

'Sure – *after* you go to the Olympics.'

'Nah. I don't want to do that anymore.'

'But what about Jakarta? We're supposed to compete in our first Olympics together.'

'I just don't think I'd make it. I mean, think about it … there were 410 Australian athletes at the Rio Games. And there are 25 million Australians. So the chance is pretty low. I worked it out. It's like one in 60,000.'

There's something wrong with Olivia's argument but it takes me a minute to work it out. Then I remember Matt's example with Usain Bolt.

'But your chance isn't the same as everyone else's in Australia,' I say. 'You have more chance than my dad. And way more chance than my nana, who is seventy and doesn't take sport seriously. Anyway, you can achieve anything you want to if you try hard enough.'

We're at the school gate now. 'Listen,' says Olivia. 'I don't want to go to the Olympics anymore. Just move on, Vivian.'

I don't want to move on. I don't want to go to the Olympics without Olivia.

On Saturday, I help Dad wash the car. We talk race tactics. He tells me I should pace myself and not go out too fast.

'Really?' I say.

'Yeah, lots of other kids will go out too hard and then drop off.'

'That's what Olivia did in the school cross country.'

'There'll be lots of fast runners at the district race, so make sure you don't wreck yourself early so you can finish strong.'

Talking about the race is making me nervous.

Dad turns on the car radio. We listen to a show called *The Sports Report* on the community radio station. A man and a woman on the show are talking about local sports events, but they sound like they're talking about the Olympics or the AFL grand final or something.

They talk about the F-grade Bendigo tennis final. Long Gully were beaten by Kangaroo Flat and didn't win a single set.

'It was their baseline game that let Long Gully down, ultimately.'

'And their short game.'

'And their serving.'

'And their unforced errors.'

'Their inability to hit the ball over the net may have played a role too.'

It's a bit mean, but I can't help laughing.

On the morning of the district cross country, Mum drives me to Gap Hill Primary School for the race. Mum's not sure if she can watch, unfortunately, because she has an important meeting with human resources about the new staff partnership agreement. Whatever that means.

She drops me off at the gate and I walk in by myself. I'm glad I'm only visiting for one day. I wouldn't like to come here every day. For one thing, I've heard that their toilets stink.

Gap Hill Primary School is a huge red brick building with white windows and arches. In the middle is a clock tower with a spire on top. I wonder if kids are ever allowed to climb up to the top of the tower. That would be amazing. Our school, Wallaby Flat Primary, has no stairs – we even have ramps up to the portables. We also have a state-of-the-art recycling station, and a worm farm complex that just looks like a lot of bins.

I'm supposed to meet Alex and the others from Wallaby Flat Primary on the oval. I don't know where that is, so I follow a group of kids who look like they know where they're going.

I spot Sam waiting with Alex. Madeline arrives after me and then also Aryo from grade six. We're only a small team – some of the other schools have brought heaps more kids than we have.

Alex tells us it's time for a warm-up jog.

'Shouldn't we save our energy?' asks Sam.

'No, you'll run faster if you warm up first,' says Alex.

We jog around the school perimeter with Alex.

It's exciting to be running with someone who nearly went to the Commonwealth Games. Alex chats while we run, maybe to take our minds off our pre-race nerves. He says he would have liked to bring more kids from our school, but some of our teachers were annoyed about us missing too many days of school for sport.

'You mean Matt?' I ask.

Alex won't say, but it's definitely Matt.

When we get back to the start line there's still fifteen minutes until the race begins. The waiting is horrible.

Madeline says she needs to go to the toilet so the two of us go together. At the toilet block we join the queue behind some girls from Gap Hill. They don't say hello, even though we are the visitors and they should be being nice to us.

'Did you see those freaks jogging around the school with their teacher?' says one of the girls. She has a long dark ponytail.

'Yeah, the Wallaby Flat kids.'

'You know what my brother calls them?'

'What?' The other girls lean in to listen.

She whispers something to them. I don't hear it, but I don't need to. I know what they call us. We call them Crap Hill but that's not as bad.

The girls see us and nudge each other. 'Oh,

sorry!' says the girl with the long dark ponytail. 'I was only joking. You looked *really* good running with your teacher.'

Toilets flush and three cubicle doors swing open practically at the same time. The Crap Hill girls go in.

After we finally get to use the toilets, Madeline and I walk back to the oval together.

'Those toilets really smelled,' says Madeline. 'I don't know how they stand it.'

I agree.

Alex tells me it's time to go to the start line. Madeline and Sam won't run in the same race as me because they split everyone up into boys and girls and by age.

Madeline and Sam say, 'Good luck.' I don't want to leave them, but I walk to the start line where the other girls are crowding around. I'm not brave enough to push to the front like Olivia did so I stand at the back.

A teacher from Gap Hill comes to the front and gives instructions, but I can't hear her properly, and anyway, I can't concentrate because I'm so nervous.

Finally, the teacher stops talking. Then another voice says, 'On your marks!' Then there's a loud whistle.

The race starts, but I'm barely moving because I'm waiting for the kids in front to get going. And once we finally set off I can only jog because I'm stuck behind slow pokes. One of them is running about as fast as Calvin does. I weave between kids to overtake – and finally, I can run properly.

Up ahead the race leaders are already far in front. The girl with the long dark ponytail is with them. I want to catch up, but then I remember Dad's advice about not going out too fast.

I concentrate on staying beside a girl wearing a yellow polo top. She's sounding puffed out already, so if I stay with her, I won't go too fast too early.

We run off the oval and cross a small road. An adult wearing a fluorescent pink vest holds up a stop sign for the car waiting for us to run past.

We run to the big park where we'll do a lap before running back. I've come to this park lots of times for picnics and one time we came to watch *The Wind in the Willows.*

Up ahead the race leaders are still going strong.

The girl in the yellow polo top falls behind and when I look back, she's walking.

We come around the end of the park and along the other side. I pass a teacher who shouts, 'Good work! Only one kilometre to go!'

I thought we'd only just begun, but the race is

nearly over. I speed up and overtake people in front.

I'm back to the road and to the teacher with the stop sign. When I pass her she says, 'Good work. Nearly there.'

I'm sweating now and I'm glad I'm wearing my new deodorant.

I can see the oval, but I realise it's too late. People have crossed the finish line. I can't catch up to them if they've finished.

One person in front of me is still close enough to catch. I gain steadily on them until we are running side by side. Alex is near the finish line and shouts, 'Good work, Vivian!'

I spot my mum waving at me.

I throw myself forward at the line.

Leaning with my hands on my knees, I try to get my breath back. Someone hands me a bottle of water.

The girl with the long dark ponytail is talking to her friends. She's smiling a lot, so she probably won.

Alex comes over. 'What happened? You finished very strong, but you were a little behind your usual pace.'

'Yeah, it wasn't as far as I thought.' I take a sip from my bottle. 'When they said one kilometre to go, I couldn't believe it.'

'You could have gone faster?'

'Maybe. I wasn't really trying for the first part.'

'We'll have to work on that before the regional final.'

'I'm going to the regional final?'

'You just made the top ten. You had a good lunge to the finish there.'

Madeline says, 'Well done, Vivian!'

I can't stop smiling. I only came tenth, but I qualified for the final, and that's what counts because it means I get to race again.

'Where's Sam?' I ask.

'His race is just about to start,' says Alex. 'We should go watch.'

The three of us are about to walk to the start line again, when I hear someone yell, 'We need an ambulance!'

Alex and I turn to look. There's a commotion where the spectators are, and I can't see what's going on because too many people are crowding around. But I know. It's Mum. It's happened again.

I run and then push in. Someone tries to pull me away and says, 'Give her room.'

'She's my mum!' I say, and they let me in.

Her skirt has ridden up and everyone can see her white legs. I pull her skirt down to make sure people can't see her knickers.

Mum opens her eyes. 'Where am I?' she says, and then shuts her eyes again.

By the time the ambulance arrives Mum is sitting up drinking a cup of tea and she seems much better. She keeps apologising for causing a fuss and everyone keeps telling her not to be silly.

Dad arrives to drive us home, so I don't get to go back to school in the minibus. Dad wants to take Mum straight to the hospital, but she won't let him. After all, she says, the ambulance people weren't worried. They thought she stood in the sun for too long, and she hadn't had anything to eat today because she was so busy with the staff partnership agreement and the HR people, who are being a nightmare.

I try to lighten the mood by telling Mum and Dad I've qualified for the regional cross country final. I tell them about how I only just made the top ten, and how I only just managed to overtake someone at the very end.

Mum says it was very exciting watching us sprint for the finish. It was the last thing she saw before she fell over.

When we get home, Dad insists Mum goes to her room to lie down. She agrees, which means she must still be feeling sick because she usually says that daytime rests are for toddlers.

I go to my room as well. I'm restless, even though I should be tired. I wish I could go for another run, but I need to recover.

The regional cross country final is a whole month away. It's a good thing because I'll have time to train, but a bad thing because I don't want to wait that long for my next race.

9

COACHING

I'm worried about going to school the day after the district cross country because Sam might have told everyone about Mum fainting. Daniel would be awful about it.

I meet Olivia at the bottom of the hill.

'How did you go?' she asks.

'I came tenth.'

'I'm sorry,' she says and puts her hand on my shoulder.

'No, that's good. I've qualified for the regional cross country final.' I tell Olivia about the race, how I nearly came eleventh.

'Sounds like a dream come true.'

'It is. Except cross country isn't an Olympic sport.'

'If you're good at cross country, you can run middle-distance track. Or maybe you'll be a marathon runner like Alex. Except *you'll* actually go to the Commonwealth Games.' Olivia starts to walk up the hill. 'How did Sam go?' she asks.

'I'm not sure. I didn't get to watch his race,' I say. 'What with one thing and another.'

Liza is at the table when we arrive. I tell her about the district cross country and about how I nearly came eleventh but then I came tenth. I explain that I don't know how Sam went in his race yet.

'You keep going on about Sam,' says Olivia. 'Do you like him or something?'

Olivia is the one who used to like Sam. She admitted it at her birthday party last year. But now Olivia says she doesn't like anyone.

'I don't like him. I'm just reporting on the results for Wallaby Flat.'

'You didn't mention Madeline or Aryo.'

'They're not from our class,' I say quickly because I don't want Olivia to start going on about me and Sam.

Olivia raises one eyebrow, and she only does that when she's suspicious. Luckily, the song plays so we have to stop debating and get to class.

Olympic history is our first lesson in the

morning. We learn about the countries that have hosted an Olympic Games. There has *never* been an Olympic Games in Africa. I don't think that's fair. The continents should take it in turns.

After history, Matt tells us about how debating teams work. The person who speaks first is supposed to define the terms in the debate. For example, what does 'Olympic Games' mean. The second person rebuts the other team's arguments, defends their team's definitions and makes positive points. Rebutting means you give reasons why what the other team said isn't true. The third person does more rebutting and summarises the whole thing.

Matt gives us time to work in our debate groups. Team Spain get together and the three of us discuss which order we'll go in. I want to go second or third because I want to say why the other team's arguments are wrong. Liza says she doesn't mind going first, so I will go second and Calvin will go last. We get sorted just as the bell rings for recess.

I'm slow getting my muesli bar out of my bag and the others go without me. It's just me and Sam left in the classroom.

'Is your mum okay?' he asks.

'Yeah, she's fine. She faints all the time.'

'So she's alright?'

'I think so. She's supposed to go to the doctors again today.' I change the subject. 'How did your race go? I'm sorry I missed it.'

'Good,' Sam says. 'I get to go to the regional final too.'

'Really?'

'Yep. I came tenth.' Sam takes an apple out of his bag, throws it in the air and catches it again. I can't risk that sort of thing with fruit.

'I came tenth too!' I say.

'I know, we're twins!' He looks at me and smiles.

I have to look away, but I'm smiling too.

I run down the portable ramp and go to meet the others.

A week later, Madeline, Sam and I are waiting for Alex at the school's back gate.

The way it happened was this. Alex called Mum and said he would give me extra running coaching before the regional cross country final. He said, 'Vivian has a bit of ability that we could develop'. I think having *a bit of ability* is the same as having *potential*, but it doesn't sound as good. Doing the coaching by myself would be weird, so Alex said he would run a special training program with other kids as well. But only Sam and Madeline wanted to join. Madeline didn't make the regional final, unfortunately, but she has her eyes on next year.

So that's why the three of us are here. Sam is eating an apple. He eats the core as well, which I've never seen anyone do before.

Alex arrives wearing black tights instead of tracksuit pants. It is hard to stop staring.

'Why are you wearing stockings?' asks Sam.

'They're not stockings. They're running tights. They support your joints and muscles and help you recover.'

'They do look like stockings, though,' says Madeline.

'They're very comfortable. Let's move on,' says Alex.

We jog around the oval. Then Alex takes us through some warm-ups. First, we swing our arms around in the air then rotate our ankles. Then we rotate our hips. I can't look at Sam while I'm doing this. I'm glad no one else in the school can see us.

Madeline giggles. I can't help it, I'm giggling too, and then so is Sam. Alex says he can't see what's so funny, which is sad.

Next, we do sprints. We run as fast as we can across the oval. Sam runs flat out. Alex tells him it's not supposed to be a race and he should only put in about 80 per cent effort. I think Sam put in at least 90 per cent. We walk back and then do it two more times.

For the next part, Alex explains that we'll run a lap of the oval as fast as we can and then jog for half a lap. Then we'll repeat that five times.

We run together for the first couple of laps. Sam and Madeline race each other at the end and I finish just behind them.

Before our last lap Alex says, 'Right, guys, I want to see who's been foxing. This is the last rep so just give it everything you have.'

I run fast. I drop Sam and Madeline before we even reach the first set of goalposts. Alex stays with me.

'Keep going strong to the finish,' he says. I might be imagining it, but he runs a bit faster and I keep up with him. I don't know if I can keep running at this pace, but when we go past the second set of goalposts, I know it's not far to go. I can make it.

Alex speeds up again and I stay with him to the end. When we finish, I'm exhausted. Madeline and Sam are just running past the second goalposts.

'Now that was proper running,' says Alex. 'The point of interval training is to try as hard as you can.'

‘I’m not good at sprinting,’ I say. ‘I’m better when it’s further.’

‘Intervals will help you with your distance running. But you can’t hang back with the others or you won’t get the benefit.’

Madeline and Sam finally finish, and Alex gives them a minute to recover before we jog another lap together.

After the coaching session is over, Madeline, Sam and I wait in the carpark for our parents. We talk about how hard Alex made us run, and I’m a bit surprised by how tired I am because I often run five kilometres, and this was only a few laps of the oval.

Sam asks if we’ve ever listened to *The Sports Report* on the radio.

‘Yes!’ I say. ‘I heard it the other day.’

‘It’s so funny,’ he says.

‘What is it?’ asks Madeline.

Sam explains how they cover local sporting events and make fun of the teams.

‘I don’t think that sounds funny,’ says Madeline. ‘They’re being mean about people trying their hardest.’

I imagine how I would feel if *The Sports Report* covered my first soccer game. Or the time I froze on the beam during a meet and Pat, the gymnastics coach, had to lift me off. It was bad enough having people there see me embarrass myself, let alone having it broadcast to the entire Central Goldfields region.

'Nah,' says Sam. 'It's okay. The teams they cover are in on the joke. You're not supposed to take it seriously.'

Mum arrives, and I have to say goodbye to Sam and Madeline.

Mum and I drive to Noah's school to pick him up after band practice. I think about running training. It's funny that I haven't been friends with Sam before because we actually have a lot in common. And even though he's friends with Daniel, he doesn't call me 'Slitherin' Vivian' like Daniel does.

Noah gets into the front passenger seat with his trumpet. 'What are you doing here?' he says.

'I had running coaching.'

'Who with?'

'Alex.'

'What are you doing that for?'

'To improve my running.' I'm starving hungry now. I look in my bag, but I don't have any food left.

'Why do you need coaching for that? You put one foot in front of the other. I hope we're not paying for this, Mum?'

'It's free, unlike your trumpet lessons,' I say.

'At least there's a point to the trumpet.'

'What's the point of the trumpet?'

Noah turns around to look at me. 'It's art. Not just running around in a circle.'

'That's enough, you two,' says Mum. 'Let's agree to honour all fields of human endeavour.'

'Including homeopathy?' asks Noah, because he knows she hates that.

Mum ignores him because that is the best policy. I also ignore him because I'm too hungry to argue.

'Anyway, does that mean I can go to music camp even if I don't play footy?' asks Noah.

'I think so,' says Mum.

'What about Dad?' I ask.

'It'll be fine,' says Mum. 'We'll talk to him.'

After tea, Mum, Dad and Noah have a serious talk in the kitchen. I lie on my bed and listen. I can hear most of what they're saying because they left the kitchen door open.

Noah says Dad is ashamed of him for being overweight. Dad says playing sport is about staying healthy and making friends; it's definitely not about losing weight, and anyway, Noah always liked playing footy so why was he quitting now?

Noah won't change his mind and Mum is on his side, so at the end of the conversation they agree that Noah can go to music camp even though he's not going to play football this year. I'm happy for Noah because he would be miserable if he didn't go to music camp.

But I'm worried about him too. I want Noah to be healthy and have friends.

We have sport with Alex first thing. We play T-ball. My team bats first. I get run out before I make it to first base, so I have been no use to my team.

Daniel bats last for our team. The bases are loaded with Olivia on third, Calvin on second and Holly on first. She's been there for a while but hasn't been brave enough to leave.

Daniel smashes the ball and everyone runs. Olivia gets home easily. Nasrin is fielding, but ever since she fell on sports day her ankle has been funny, so she can't run as fast as she used to.

It looks like everyone will get home. Daniel overtakes Holly and Calvin on his way and gets home next. Holly overtakes Calvin as well and makes it home. Nasrin finally gets to the ball and throws it to Sam at home base. She is a good thrower at least.

Calvin is out.

Daniel is furious at Calvin and says, 'You run like a girl, mate!'

As usual, Alex doesn't hear Daniel and he doesn't get in trouble.

At lunchtime, Liza says she has had enough of Daniel. 'He's so mean to Calvin and it's not fair. Anyway, you two are the fastest runners in the school. Daniel *wishes* he could run like a girl.'

'He's always like that,' I say.

'Yeah, we just ignore him,' says Olivia.

'It's the best policy,' I add.

'Well, ignoring him isn't stopping him!' Liza's face is bright red. She's really angry.

'But what can we do about it?' I say.

'We should start a campaign,' says Liza.

'How do you do that?'

Liza looks like she's had a great idea. 'When the nurses' strike was on, they made badges! Mum wore hers every day.'

'Did that help?'

'They got the pay rise.'

So the three of us go to the library and ask to borrow the school badge maker which usually only comes out for the fete. The school librarian, Dimitra, doesn't want to let us borrow it, but after we explain our plan, she agrees.

After lunch, Liza, Olivia and I go into the classroom wearing our new badges. They say: 'I Run Like a Girl'.

Liza, Olivia and I stand at the doorway and hand badges out to people coming back into the classroom.

Daniel and Sam walk in together. Daniel looks at the badges and says, 'I don't get it, Olivian. You guys are really good runners.'

'That's our point,' says Olivia.

Daniel shakes his head and doesn't take a badge. I offer one to Sam and he takes it and pins it to his shirt. Daniel calls him something rude. Sam shrugs.

In the afternoon, we have group work for our class debates. Matt tells us to work on our rebuttal. We're supposed to think of arguments that the other team might make, and then think of arguments for why they're wrong. I'm very glad we have Calvin on our team because Liza and I can't think of any reasons to cancel the Olympics.

REASONS WHY THE OLYMPIC GAMES SHOULD BE CANCELLED:
Too expensive
Bad for the environment
Too many drugs in sport
Not good for homeless people

Unnecessary infrastructure
No netball in the Olympics

We add the last one for Liza, but I can tell Calvin doesn't think it's a very good argument.

On Saturday, I go for a run but make sure I'm home before 10 am. Mum is listening to a podcast and unpacking the dishwasher when I come into the kitchen.

'Can I listen to *The Sports Report*?' I ask.

'I just need to finish this job.'

'What if I do it for you?'

'I suppose that's okay.'

Mum leaves the kitchen and takes her boring podcast about the history of dictionaries with her.

I turn the radio on and switch the channel to 3PT. *The Sports Report* is just starting.

I'm feeling really exhausted after my run, so I get a glass of water and sit at the kitchen table to listen. Their special guest is the captain of the Golden Square Petanque Club. They keep talking about his big silver balls, and I can't stop giggling. Along the way, I actually learn something about how to play petanque, which is nice. I imagine Sam is listening too, and it almost feels like he's in the room with me.

Then Mum comes back and wants to know why I haven't finished unpacking the dishwasher. She doesn't understand how important recovery is after training.

10

HEALTHY ME, HEALTHY YOU

A week later, first thing in the morning, Matt tells us we won't be doing sport with Alex.

'Not fair!' yells Sam.

'Settle down,' says Matt.

A rumbling sound comes from outside. Our whole class looks out the window. A truck is driving into the school and onto the asphalt area. And it's not the mobile library.

Principal Faye is wearing a fluorescent yellow vest and gesturing to the truck driver.

'Sit down, everybody!' yells Matt.

Most people go back to their seats except Calvin. 'What's the truck for?' he says.

'I will not be telling you anything until everyone is sitting down and being quiet. That means *everyone.*'

'Sit down, Calvin!' yells Sam.

Calvin comes back to his chair.

'This morning, instead of doing sport with Alex, you'll be visiting the Health Education van to do their program, Healthy Me, Healthy You,' says Matt. 'I've been telling you about this for weeks, so I guess you haven't been listening. We're very lucky to have this opportunity, so I hope you'll be on your best behaviour. Now, until the van is ready, I would like everyone to concentrate on probability.'

There's a lot of talking while we work because everyone is excited about the Healthy Me, Healthy You program. I would be more excited if we were missing maths instead of sport. Matt tells us off because he says we are just making noise, and not productive noise.

Finally, Alex comes in and says we can make our way quietly out to the basketball court.

We line up on the asphalt. Once we're all quiet we walk up the metal steps into the van. Inside it's big enough for everyone to sit on the floor, which is carpeted with scratchy grey squares. We all get to choose a cushion to sit on. I choose a red cushion with yellow dots.

The woman in charge of the Healthy Me, Healthy You program is called Tamara. She has very curly hair and her bracelets of wooden beads make a relaxing *tap tap* noise when she moves around.

Tamara tells us to lie on the floor and look up at the ceiling. The Health Education van is surprisingly spacious, but it feels smaller once everyone lies down. Calvin's foot is in my face at first, so I move to the left. Then Sam's feet are in my face. I will ignore that.

Tamara turns off the lights. The ceiling is dark but gradually stars appear above us. It's like being at the planetarium, only rectangular.

A voice on the speakers talks about how our bodies are made of materials that were once in stars. We are all stars. Jingling music like wind chimes plays in the background. I forget about the rest of my class as I watch the beautiful sky above me. The universe is an amazing place.

Eventually the stars and the music fade away and the lights come back on. We sit up and Tamara asks how we felt when we were looking at the stars.

A few people put their hands up, but Tamara says we don't have to put our hands up to talk. We just need to respect each other, listen and take turns.

'I felt relaxed,' says Liza.

'That's great. I'm glad you experienced that.

How did other people feel?' asks Tamara.

'Peaceful,' I say without even putting my hand up.

Tamara nods. 'That's great.'

'Sleepy.'

'Calm.'

'Excited,' says Calvin. I bet because he wants to be an astronomer.

'How about you?' Tamara asks Holly.

Holly looks at her feet. 'Um. Anxious.'

'Why anxious?'

'Because the universe is so big and we're all going to die and be completely insignificant.'

Holly is always being negative.

Tamara isn't annoyed at Holly, though. She nods and says, 'Those are big thoughts. Thank you for sharing.'

Next, Tamara gets us to break into two groups, boys and girls, and write down things that feel good. Our group puts: eating ice-cream, sitting in the sun, running, winning, trying hard, playing with puppies or kittens, haircuts.

The boys are giggling a lot, so Liza looks at their list to see what's so funny. They've written a rude word. They try to scrub it out, but they're not even in trouble because Tamara says that it's fine for us to enjoy our bodies in private.

Next, we make a list of things that make us feel bad. We put: being left out, sunburn, banging your elbow, losing.

Olivia suggests 'running'.

'Running doesn't feel bad,' I say.

'It does,' she says. 'It hurts.'

It hurts sometimes, but it's worth it.

'Blunt instrument trauma to the head,' suggests Holly.

We laugh.

After we share our lists, Tamara plays us a film. We lie down again to watch it projected on the roof. It is so excellent. When I grow up, I'm going to have my television on the ceiling.

The show is about smoking and drinking and about how they make you feel bad. Smoking makes you cough, gives you asthma, makes you smell, makes you worse at sport and gives you cancer. Drinking alcohol makes you feel sick, throw up, lose brain cells, fight with people, feel sad, and also gives you cancer.

After the film, Tamara asks if any of us have tried smoking. She says we won't get in trouble if we say yes, but no one says yes. Tamara says lots of kids try smoking or alcohol in high school because of the peer pressure.

After that we break up in groups and plan a

puppet show about how to handle peer pressure.

I go in a group of three with Liza and Olivia. In our show the wombat tries to get the platypus to smoke. He says it will make the platypus cool. The platypus says he doesn't want to, and plays handball with the echidna instead. Tamara says it is a great strategy.

At the end, we lie down again and watch the ceiling. We watch an animation with a catchy song about how bad smoking and drinking will make us feel. It's the kind of song that makes me want to go for a run because it's so inspiring.

When we walk down the steps of the Health Education van, everyone is excited. The bell rings for recess but the whole class stays on the basketball courts talking. We all agree that we will never smoke, even if people peer pressure us at high school.

Alex comes over and asks if we enjoyed the Healthy Me, Healthy You program. We say it was great and we loved it. Calvin says his favourite bit was the stars, Liza liked the puppets and Olivia wants to work in the Health Education van when she grows up. I assume she'll do that in her holidays from being a sports scientist. My favourite bit was the song.

*

After school, I go for a run. When I get to the river I turn around and run all the way to the main road. I think about the Healthy Me, Healthy You program. It is so good that no one in our class will ever try smoking or drinking. We have great things ahead of us. Sam is going to play for Collingwood, I'm going to the Olympics, Liza is going to play netball for the Vixens, Calvin is going to be an astronaut, Olivia is going to be a sports scientist. I used to think Daniel would go to jail, but after today I want everyone in my class to do well, so I hope he doesn't. I don't know what Holly will do, but there must be something out there for people who like sitting down a lot.

I sing the Healthy Me, Healthy You song in my head and that makes me run faster.

When I arrive back from my run, tea is ready. Tonight, it's broccoli pasta. Mum is always telling me that broccoli is a superfood but I am suspicious because superfoods usually aren't cheap like broccoli.

Mum asks me what I did at school. I say we had the Healthy Me, Healthy You program.

'What did they talk to you about?'

'Smoking and stuff.'

'I assume *not* smoking,' says Dad.

'Yeah, of course.'

'Did they have puppets at the end?' says Noah.

'How did you know about that?'

'We did it when I was in primary school.'

Noah has always done everything first. He thinks it makes him special or something, but it doesn't – it just makes him older.

After tea, Noah and I clean up the kitchen.

'What are you humming?' asks Noah.

'Nothing.'

'It's that song, isn't it?' says Noah. He sings, 'If you smoke you're gonna choke, and if you drink you're gonna sink.' Noah sounds good, even when he's making fun of a song.

'It's stuck in my head.'

'It's such a cheesy song.' Noah stacks plates in the dishwasher too close together.

I change the topic. 'Do people in high school really smoke?'

Noah says, 'Yeah,' like it's completely obvious.

'But why?'

'I suppose they want to.'

'But smoking gives you cancer and makes your lungs clog up like a sponge filled with slime.'

'I suppose.'

'You can't run as fast if you smoke.'

Noah snorts. 'Not everyone wants to spend their life mindlessly putting one foot in front of the other so they can run slightly faster than some other jock.'

Noah puts a big pot in the dishwasher that I know will jam the spinner so it won't rotate properly. I don't say anything because giving Noah advice is never a good idea. I start wiping the bench instead. 'That's not what running is about,' I say.

'What is it about then?'

I stop wiping and think about it. Running is about not knowing if I can do something and then doing it. It's the fun of overtaking someone who's trying their hardest but can't run as fast as me. It's about controlling my body and making it do what I tell it to. It's feeling completely relaxed when it's over. It's being my best and knowing I'm alive.

I think Noah takes being alive for granted, but he shouldn't. We are all so lucky to be here. Mum had a brother, Liam, who I never met. He died suddenly at footy training when he was sixteen.

I can't explain any of that to Noah, so I just say, 'Anyway, no one from *my* class will smoke.'

Noah slams the dishwasher shut. 'Yes, they will.'

'No, they won't.'

'Everyone says they won't after the Health Education van comes. But they do.'

'Have you?' I ask.

'What do you reckon?'

There's no way Noah would be that silly. 'No,' I say.

He laughs.

Noah goes to his room because he thinks we're finished. I stay in the kitchen, rearranging the dishwasher so that it will actually clean the dishes. I feel like crying. Noah is smoking and not looking after his health. I might lose my brother, just like Mum did.

11

REGIONAL FINAL

On the day of the regional cross country final, we meet at school at seven in the morning to get an early start. My race is at 10 am sharp. We're driving to St Arnaud in Alex's car.

Sam is waiting in the school parking lot when I arrive. I wave at him and he waves back.

Kim, the grade six teacher and You Yangs house leader, is coming with us as well. As we pull out of the carpark she says, 'So, are you guys excited?'

'Yes,' say Sam and I together.

'You don't sound very excited.'

'I'm a bit nervous,' I say.

Kim says she remembers what it's like. She once went to the school athletics national finals for high jump in Malaysia.

'What happened?' I ask.

'I came third. Then the next year I didn't make it to the finals.'

'Why not?' I ask.

'I stopped growing and the other kids didn't. I went from being the tallest to the shortest girl in the class in one year.'

'But if you'd kept working at it, you could have made it to the Olympics, or at least the Commonwealth Games,' I say. 'You can achieve anything if you work hard enough.'

Suddenly I remember that Alex didn't make it to the Commonwealth Games and I feel bad. I hope I haven't reminded him of his failure.

'Sadly, work is a poor substitute for talent,' says Kim.

'Luckily Vivian has both,' says Alex.

'The important thing is to do your best,' says Kim.

I roll my eyes, which luckily Kim can't see from the front seat.

'And it's important for you to go out hard, Vivian,' says Alex. 'You've got the ability. You just need to trust yourself.'

'But shouldn't I pace myself so I can finish strong?'

'Not if you want to get a good result. Go out fast and then try to hang on.'

I nod. I like the sound of his plan.

'What about me?' asks Sam.

'Just do your best, mate,' says Alex.

Alex and Kim talk to each other in the front of the car. It's very interesting to listen to. Apparently, someone is always putting roadblocks in the way of the sports program. It's probably Matt.

'Do you want to play car cricket?' Sam asks.

I say yes. I have a fantastic innings and score 100, which I've never done before.

The carpark is nearly full when we arrive, but Alex's car is really little so he manages to squeeze it into a spot next to a tree.

We make our way to the assembly point in the middle of the oval. I'm glad Kim, Alex and Sam are with me because I would have no idea where to go or what to do without them. Some schools have tents with the school's logo and their students wear matching running uniforms. Sam and I are in our normal school uniforms, but I think that's okay because they are designed for sport.

There's a lady sitting at the registration table, and Alex tells her our names and that we're from Wallaby Flat Primary School. She gives Sam and me numbers to wear. Kim pins my number to the back of my shirt and I pin one on the front. I'm also wearing my 'I Run Like a Girl' badge because I promised Liza and Olivia that I would.

Alex shows me a map of the course. It's a big loop starting and finishing on the oval.

'What if I get lost?'

'You can't get lost,' he says. 'They have marshals all along the way to tell you where to go.'

My race is scheduled first but there's still half an hour until it starts, so Alex takes us for a warm-up jog. Kim comes too and tries to chat with us, but I'm too nervous to talk, and Sam isn't saying much either.

At least this time I don't feel embarrassed because heaps of other people are jogging around too. Some people are even doing weird running where they pull their knees up super high like football umpires.

The regional finals are bigger than the district finals because there are secondary schoolkids here too. Some of the older girls are wearing crop tops and undies like the athletes in the Olympics.

'Hey, there's the Gap Hill gang!' says Alex. He waves at a teacher and we go over to them. Six kids from Crap Hill are in the regional final. One of them is the girl with the long dark ponytail who teased us at the district cross country race.

Alex, Kim and the Crap Hill teacher chat to each other. Then they join us for the rest of the warm-up jog.

It turns out that the girl with the long dark ponytail is called Elisa.

'How did you get here today?' she asks me.

'Car. What about you guys?'

'Minibus.'

Elisa and I line up together for the portaloos before the race. The kids from other districts don't talk to us, and Elisa and I agree that they are snobs.

After using the portaloos, which really do smell, Elisa and I go back to the Gap Hill group.

I hear a loudspeaker announcement saying that competitors in the girls' eleven-year-old cross country regional final should assembly at the start line.

Kim wishes me good luck.

Alex tells me to push into the front at the start line. 'Go hard or go home,' he says.

Sam says, 'Go, Bendigo!' to Elisa and me. Being from Bendigo is the important thing today, it's not about specific schools.

Elisa and I go to the start line and try to get to the front like Alex said. I only make it to the second row because the girls at the front won't make room for me. They stick out their elbows and I can't get past them.

We wait for a long time.

The girl beside me says, 'Haven't seen you

before. Have you done much racing this season?'

'Just school cross country.'

'Oh. So you don't run with Athletics Victoria?'

'No.'

'Okay. Interesting.'

Suddenly everyone leans forward. I lean forward too. Someone is pushing me from behind.

'On your marks.'

The sound of the starter's pistol gives me a fright but we're running at last. No one is slowing me down this time. These girls are quick. I think they're too quick, but then I remember Alex saying, 'Go hard or go home,' and it's not home time yet.

We run across the green grass of the oval. I stay with the girls at the front. My knees feel wobbly, but I know that feeling will pass.

I look over and see Elisa running beside me. 'Go, Bendigo!' she says.

The leaders are pulling away so I go with them, but Elisa doesn't.

We get off the oval and onto the road. I prefer the feeling of firm ground rather than grass to run on.

About ten girls are running in a bunch just in front of me. We run around a corner. We pass a race marshal wearing a fluorescent vest who tells us to keep going straight.

'Doing well, girls!' he yells. 'Nearly there.'

We've only just begun. I don't know if he thinks he's being helpful, but he isn't.

We're running past scrubby bush and the track slopes downwards. The girls in front of me speed up, so I do too. This downhill section means there will be uphill later, but I try not to think about that.

We come to a T-intersection, and a lady calls out, 'Right!'

We get around the corner and a hill rises dauntingly ahead. A few girls slow down and I overtake them. Now I'm in a bunch at the front with four other people.

The hill goes on and on. I wish I'd done more hill training. Alex wanted to take us out for hill runs, but we weren't allowed off school property for coaching.

I count the poles as I pass. I tell myself that by the time I've passed ten poles, I'll be at the top of the hill. I concentrate on running to the next pole, then the next one, and the next one.

Ahead is a corner I can't see around. I hope the path will flatten out after that. But we turn the corner, and I realise that it doesn't. The hill keeps going up.

I chant in my head, 'Go, Bendigo! Go, Bendigo!'

Then it changes to, 'Go hard or go home. Go hard or go Bendigo!'

At the real top of the hill I'm still with the race leaders, but I'm so exhausted. The other girls make it look so easy, like they're not even trying.

A girl wearing a blue top overtakes the rest of us and sprints down the hill. I speed up, not wanting her to get too far in front.

We run past a building and then turn around a sharp corner. Blue Top is just in front of me. The marshal posted on the corner shouts, 'Nearly there!'

I've heard that before but this time it's probably true.

'One last hill and then you're home!'

Only one more hard bit. I've got this. When I get to the top of the hill, I'll be back at the oval and it will all be over. I get closer and closer to Blue Top. At the top of the hill I overtake her.

I hear someone shout, 'Go, Bendigo!' but I don't know who it is.

We're back on the oval. Sticks with colourful bunting strung between them mark out a track around the oval. We have to run all the way to the other side.

I don't like running on the grass – I feel like I'm fighting against the softness of the ground.

There are three of us running together. A girl with a blonde plait and someone wearing long white socks. I'm coming second or third. I could get a ribbon.

As we run around the bend, I look across over my shoulder and see that Blue Top is only a few metres behind.

'Looking good, Vivian. Strong to the finish!' It's Alex, standing with Kim.

My thighs hurt, my lungs ache. The other girls will sprint to the end. I don't know if I can do that. *Go hard or go home*, he said. Maybe I should have gone home.

'Go, Vivian!' calls another voice from the spectators. It sounds like Sam.

I remember the times we ran around the oval at school together, with Alex making me run faster. I thought about stopping then, but I never did.

Long Socks picks up the pace. I go with her.

I won't let Long Socks beat me. I run a little bit faster. So does she. We're side by side.

It will be over after I count to ten. I promise myself. I speed up one more time to the finish. Long Socks doesn't stay with me. I cross the line.

I won.

PART
TWO

12

TESTS

Alex drops me off at my house and I burst through the front door holding my medal. Mum, Dad and Noah are sitting in the kitchen.

'I won!'

'That's fantastic!' says Mum.

'Congratulations!' says Dad.

'I got a gold medal *and* a trophy,' I say. 'I don't have the trophy with me because they're going to get my name engraved on it.'

'That's great!' says Mum.

I wish I could describe exactly what it was like, but I can't. I can still barely believe it happened.

Heaps of people said congratulations afterwards, including Elisa, Long Socks, Blue Top and the girl who did the Athletics Victoria races. Sam gave me a high five. The mayor of Northern Grampians shook my hand as she put the gold medal around my neck. Alex patted my shoulder and said, 'Well done,' and it was the best compliment because I knew he really meant it. Alex doesn't say things just to be nice.

We stayed to watch the older kids race. Sam and I ate our sandwiches sitting on the grass. He came 40th in his race but he didn't seem too disappointed. It was the best feeling to relax and know that we were finished while other people were still running.

On the car trip home, Kim, Sam and Alex wanted to hear every detail of the race. After I gave them a full report, I stared out the window watching the paddocks and trees speed by, feeling warm, happy and excited about the next race.

Noah stands up from the kitchen table suddenly and nearly knocks his chair over. He never says anything nice to me. He's probably just jealous so I ignore him as usual.

I sit in Noah's seat and tell Mum and Dad all about the race. I tell them how I went out as hard as I could and tried to stay with the race leaders, and how I beat Long Socks at the very end in a sprint finish.

Noah is banging cups into the dishwasher.

'Hey, Vivian, do you realise not everything's about you?' he says.

'What do you mean?'

'Have you asked how anyone else's day was?'

'We can talk about that later,' says Mum.

'Why?' I say. 'What happened today?'

'It's not important,' says Mum.

'Tell me!' Suddenly I'm worried. Mum, Dad and Noah look very serious. Something is wrong. It could be about Nana. Maybe she's sick. Or maybe Cousin Linda's cancer has come back. Or Uncle John is missing in Sydney again.

Mum pauses. 'I had some news today. But nothing's certain yet, so I don't want you to worry.'

I want to know, but I also want to run out of the room and never find out. Until Mum tells me, the news might be something little, like the car needs a new engine, or the house has termites, or we've run out of money and will have to live in a caravan.

'You know how I had those tests because I've been fainting?' says Mum.

'Yeah,' I say. She means the tests for reassurance.

'Today I went to see a specialist. It turns out that there's something wrong with my heart.'

'Do you have a hole in your heart?'

'No, it's not that. I have something called long

QT syndrome. It means that sometimes my heart beats too fast or irregularly and that's why I faint.'

'Can they fix it?'

'I can take medication.'

'And,' says Dad, 'we'll have to look after Mum and make sure she takes it easy and doesn't get too stressed. Nana's going to come and help sometimes.'

'I'll help too,' I say. 'Do you feel sick now?'

'No, no, I feel completely normal. That's what's so annoying about it.'

'That doesn't sound too bad,' I say. 'You'll be okay, Mum.'

Noah snorts. 'You wait till you google it,' he says.

'Noah!' says Mum.

'Well, it's true,' says Noah. 'It could kill you at any moment.'

'That's highly unlikely.'

'But possible,' says Noah.

'Thanks, Noah,' says Mum. 'You're really helping.' She turns to me. 'Vivian, please don't google long QT syndrome. If you have any questions, ask me about it because I've been speaking to the experts.'

'Anyway, now that we know about it, the doctors can treat it,' says Dad. 'Mum's still the same person that she was. This doesn't change who she is.'

Mum looks like she might cry, but then she says,

'You and Noah will have to have some tests too.'

'Me?'

'Yes, long QT syndrome often runs in families, unfortunately.'

'But I don't faint all the time like you do.'

'I'm sure you're fine, but the doctor said you need to be tested, just to make sure.'

For reassurance, I guess.

After tea, I use the computer then I go to Noah's room. He's practising the trumpet, but he stops playing when I push the door open and stand in his doorway.

'I looked it up,' I say.

'What did you find?'

'It says that symptoms of long QT syndrome include fainting, seizures and sudden death.'

'Yeah.'

'I didn't know death could be a symptom?'

'It's a very bad symptom. One of the worst. You need to see your doctor straight away if you experience death.'

I smile, but I can't laugh.

'Don't worry, Mum's not going to die,' Noah says.

'What about her brother Liam?' I ask. 'He died.'

'Yeah, but we don't know he had long QT.

And it was when he was heaps younger. Mum's had this for years. She'll be fine.'

Noah picks up his trumpet again. I can tell he wants me to go away so he can keep playing.

I want to go for a run but it's dark outside. And Mum says I'm not allowed until my tests rule out long QT. I don't think it's fair, but I don't want to make a big deal about it when Mum is the one who's sick.

'Um, Noah?'

'What?'

'Do you think we have it?'

'Nah, you definitely don't. Think about how fast you are. You couldn't run like that with a dodgy ticker.'

I go to my room. I feel trapped in the house. I want to get out, but I can't. I lie on my bed and try to calm down. I put my fingers on my wrist and feel my pulse. My heart beats a regular tap against my fingertips. As I get more relaxed, my heart slows down. I don't consciously do anything to keep it going; my heart beats on its own and I can't really believe that it will ever stop.

On Monday morning at assembly, Faye makes me stand on the stage in front of the whole school. Alex does a speech about how I'm the

Loddon Mallee Girls Eleven-Year-Old Regional Cross Country Champion, and that I'll be going to Melbourne for the state cross country final. I'm not actually eleven yet, but that's how it works – they put you in categories based on how old you are at the end of the year. My friends keep nudging me, but I can't look at anyone while he's talking.

Alex also mentions Sam came 40th, which is pretty good, considering.

After assembly, we have sport with Alex. For our warm-up, everyone else runs around the oval but Alex asks me to help him get the soccer balls out. He's more than capable of doing that by himself but I help him anyway.

After the warm-up that I'm not allowed to do we practise dribbling. I cannot keep the ball in front of me. Then I trip over and land on my hands and knees in the grass. A lot of people laugh. Olivia and Liza laugh too, but when I look at them, they stop.

'I am so unco,' I say as I stand up.

'At least you can run!' says Alex.

'Boring!'

'Daniel? What was that?' says Alex.

Daniel looks at the ground. 'Nothing.'

'You said something?'

Daniel looks up. His face is bright red. 'You keep going on about it, but it's not like Slitherin' Vivian's going to the Olympics.'

'Actually, Daniel, Vivian's time for the cross country final was close to the record for her age group. She might go to the Olympics.'

Daniel doesn't have anything else to say.

For the next exercise we pair up to practise kicking. I go in a pair with Liza. She's much better than I am and is very encouraging, saying things like 'Good stuff' and 'Nicely done' whenever I get something right.

I talk about myself like a sports commentator. 'It's Vivian with the ball – where will she kick it now? She's going back, she's taking a big run-up. This will be a big kick. Actually, she's missed the ball again.' I find a new way to fall over every time I kick the ball.

Liza giggles at first then she is laughing so much she can hardly chase after the ball herself. Olivia and Nasrin are next to us and they laugh too. They're laughing because I'm trying to be funny so I don't mind this time.

As we walk back from the oval to the classroom before recess, I'm still thinking about what Alex said. Becoming an Olympic athlete has been my dream for ages, but an adult thinking it might happen is new. And Alex is not just any old adult. He is an ex-semi-professional marathon runner who nearly went to the Commonwealth Games. This is the first time someone other than Olivia has believed in me.

The Olympics. *Vivian might go to the Olympics.*

I imagine the crowds in the stadium, the flashing cameras, the bright lights on the athletics track, the big television cameras capturing every moment for *millions* of people around the world to watch. And all that for running, which I love and I would do even if no one was watching.

Olivia nudges me.

'What?' I say.

'You're staring at your bag like a statue,' she says.

She's right. My schoolbag is open in front of me, but I've stopped moving. I get out my mandarin and crackers and we head to the table together.

Liza asks me questions about the cross country final while we eat. Questions like: 'What was the race course like? How big is your trophy? How will you get to Melbourne for the state final?'

I don't want to say too much about winning. I don't want them to think that I'm bragging. So I think of something else to talk about. I tell them that some of the older girls were running in undies and crop tops.

'They were in their *underwear*?' says Liza.

'Yeah, it was weird. But I guess it helps them run faster.'

'Actually,' says Olivia, 'the idea is to be more comfortable while you're running.' Olivia tells us about an article she read about high-tech fabrics. As usual, she is much more cheerful when she's teaching us things.

In the afternoon, Principal Faye comes to our portable and tells me Mum and Dad have arrived to pick me up.

'Where are you going?' whispers Olivia.

'To the doctor,' I whisper back.

'Why?'

'For a check-up.'

'You know that going to the doctor's makes you sick?'

'How?'

'The doctor's office is the most likely place to catch an infection.'

She's probably right, but I don't have any choice.

I follow Faye to her office, where Mum and Dad are waiting for me. Faye says Mum told her about her heart problem and that if I need to talk to anyone for support, I can come to her. Mum and Dad keep thanking Faye until we finally leave.

Dad is driving because Mum's not allowed in case she passes out again.

'Are you nervous?' Mum asks in the car.

'Why? Do the tests hurt?'

'No, not at all. I just thought you might be worried about it.'

'I'm not.'

I suppose I am a little bit worried, but it's like Noah said – I couldn't win the regional cross country final if there was something wrong with my heart.

Dad leaves Mum and me at the doctors and goes to the shops.

Doctor Libby asks whether I've ever fainted. I say no because I don't think it counts if you have a good reason to faint. Mum tells Doctor Libby about the needle and the school swimming carnival incidents.

'Have you ever fainted when you were running?' asks Doctor Libby.

'No.' That's true. At one of our coaching sessions, Alex said that you should go hard enough to feel dizzy and nauseas, but not so hard that you vomit or faint. Then he said he was only joking, but I don't think he was.

Doctor Libby measures my blood pressure and listens to my chest. She gives me a script to get an electrocardiogram test, which is also called an ECG.

We leave her office and cross the hall to the pathology waiting room where we take a number, but the person comes out straight away and says we can come in.

Mum asks if I want her to come in with me.

'No.'

'Are you sure?'

'No.'

'No, you're not sure, or no you don't want me to come in?'

'No, I'm not sure.'

Mum follows me in and sits on a chair against the wall. The nurse asks me to take off my top, and to lie on the bed and cover myself with the sheet. The nurse turns away as I get ready. When I'm lying down and covered, the nurse comes over again.

'How are you feeling?' she asks.

'A bit nervous,' I say. 'Will it hurt?'

'Not at all. I'm going to attach wires to you that will listen to the electrical signals that make your heart beat. It's a bit like a stethoscope. Then the machine prints out the recording for us to look at. Does that sound okay?'

'Yes.'

The nurse attaches lots of pads and wires to my

chest, arms and legs. I'm not sure what the point of the sheet is because the nurse can see everything now. Anyway, it doesn't matter because we're all girls.

The nurse turns on the machine. I lie still. At first I'm nervous, but then I realise I can't feel anything, so I relax and think about other things. I still can hardly believe I'm going to the state cross country final. Mum and Alex are going to take me to the race in Melbourne. Mum says we can drive over the Bolte Bridge on our way to Bundoora, even though technically we don't need to. Mum says we can get an ice-cream to celebrate after, even if I don't win. She says winning isn't the important thing, but I remember when I became regional champion and I want to have that feeling again. I want to win more races, even if I can't win them all.

In the car home from St Arnaud, Alex said he would write a new training program for me. He wants me to do a swimming session once a week as well as core strength exercises. I won't be allowed to start the training program until I get the results of these tests, in case I do have long QT syndrome, even though I obviously don't. Waiting is frustrating.

A voice says, 'Okay, that's done now.'

I open my eyes and the nurse is standing beside me. She takes off the wires.

'That didn't hurt at all,' I say.

'I told you so.' She smiles quickly at me.

The next day at school, Olivia and Liza are being weird and giving each other strange looks. Finally, Olivia asks me, 'How's your mum?'

'She's fine.'

'Vivian, I know,' Olivia says.

'You know what?' I ask.

'About her heart. My mum spoke to your dad at the supermarket yesterday afternoon.'

That would be right. Those two always spend ages chatting at the supermarket. Now I can't even have a normal time with my friends. Everything will be about hearts.

'It sounds pretty serious,' says Olivia.

'Kind of, but most of the time she feels fine. She's not really any different.'

'Does she have hardened arteries?' asks Liza.

'No. It's called long QT syndrome. It makes your heart beat a bit funny sometimes. But she should be fine once she starts taking her medicine.'

'What medicine?' asks Olivia.

'They're called beta-blockers. They slow your heart down or something.'

‘That sounds serious,’ Olivia says again.

‘She’s still the same person.’

‘Are you worried about her?’ asks Liza.

‘What do you think?’ I ask, and Liza looks embarrassed, so I think she gets it.

‘Well, the important thing is to stay positive,’ says Liza. ‘It’s been medically proven that staying positive makes you healthier.’

‘I don’t think there’s really any proof of that,’ says Olivia.

Luckily, Olivia and Liza don’t have a fight about it.

All this talk about Mum is making me anxious. I can feel my heart beating faster, even though I’m sitting down and not doing anything. What if it just keeps getting faster and faster and I can’t stop it?

The others want to play handball, but I’m not in the mood. I tell them that I found a new book in the library with rude pictures in it, so we go to look at that instead. At the library, I pretend someone must have borrowed it, and they believe me.

13

RESULTS

Mum and Dad pick me up from school on Friday.

'What's happening?' I ask. I know something is up.

'Your results came back today and the cardiologist wants to speak to us about them,' says Mum.

'Why can't I see Doctor Libby like normal?'

'Doctor Stanford is a heart expert,' says Dad.

'He's the same doctor I've been seeing,' says Mum. 'He's very good.'

'We're extremely lucky he's come to Bendigo,' says Dad. 'Doctor Stanford could be working anywhere. He's world-class, according to Doctor Libby.'

Dad finds a parking spot on View Street and

it's a short walk around the corner to Doctor Stanford's office.

Mum goes to the desk and talks with the receptionist. I sit on a couch in the waiting room and kick my legs against the cushions until Dad tells me to stop.

The magazines piled up on the little table next to my chair are all about the Kardashians, and none are about sport.

This room has lots of plants. I don't like the ones with the dark furry leaves because they remind me of hairy spiders. A little cactus sits on the middle of the windowsill. It's almost a perfect sphere covered in white spikes. That's the plant I would choose. It wouldn't need much watering.

A man comes into the waiting room and says, 'Vivian?'

I thought a top cardiologist would be ancient, but he looks younger than Mum and Dad. He has brown wavy hair and very white teeth.

'Hello, Vivian. I'm Doctor Stanford,' he says. 'It's nice to meet you.'

'Hello,' I say.

We walk into his office and he gestures at the chairs in front of his desk.

Doctor Stanford talks to Mum and Dad. He says a lot of things that we already know, like how

Mum has been diagnosed with long QT and how I've been tested as well. I want him to get to the point and tell us about my results.

'As you know Vivian underwent a twelve-lead ECG last week. The results show an elongated QT interval. And the elongation is quite pronounced with a corrected QT interval of five hundred and fifty milliseconds.'

The doctor pauses. I'm not sure if he's taking a break, or if he's finished talking.

The clock on his wall ticks very loudly.

'Does that mean Vivian has long QT syndrome?' asks Dad.

'That would be consistent with the clinical findings and family history.'

I turn to Dad. 'Does that mean *yes*?'

'I think so,' he says.

Dad looks very worried and that makes me feel worse.

'From Vivian's ECG, long QT type 1 is indicated. A genetic test can confirm that if you decide to proceed with testing. In the meantime, we need to develop a treatment plan for Vivian.'

Mum makes a funny gasping noise, then coughs. I try to catch her eye, but she keeps looking at the doctor.

Doctor Stanford keeps talking to Mum and Dad

about beta-blockers, ECGs, genetic counselling and lifestyle modifications. I understand what most of the words mean on their own, but I don't understand what any of it means together.

Mum asks what we should do in the meantime, before I get the treatment plan. The doctor says I should avoid stress, swimming and competitive sports.

'Like netball?' I say.

The doctor looks at me for the first time. 'Certainly netball. But any strenuous sport. Cardiac events and syncope are highly associated with exercise for people with type 1 long QT.'

'What's syncope?' I ask.

'Fainting,' Mum says.

The doctor continues. 'Vivian can do gentle exercise such as walking or even jog at a comfortable pace.'

'What's the definition of a comfortable pace?' asks Mum.

'She shouldn't be too exerted. If she can easily carry out a conversation, that's a good pace. If she can't, she needs to slow down or walk.'

I can't carry out a conversation when I'm running fast. That's the whole point, to be out of breath, absolutely at the limit.

'What about the state cross country final?

I can't jog that at a comfortable pace. I'd come last!'

The doctor keeps talking to Mum and Dad. 'I understand Vivian has been a keen competitive runner. She may benefit from counselling as we develop her treatment plan. There may be a difficult period of adjustment where she will need to modify her expectations and develop realistic future goals.'

In the car on the way home I stare out the window. I don't believe what the doctor told us. It doesn't seem right. It doesn't add up. It doesn't make any sense.

'What about Noah and Dad?' I ask.

'What about us?' asks Dad.

'Do you have long QT syndrome? Do you have to avoid strenuous exercise?'

'I don't have a history of long QT in my family,' says Dad. 'And Noah hasn't had any symptoms and his ECG results were okay.'

Noah doesn't even like sport, except footy, and he quit that too. He wouldn't care if he had heart disease and he'll probably get it anyway because he practically admitted that he smokes.

Mum turns around to look at me. 'After I get my genetic results in a couple of months, you two might be tested as well. But we need to talk to the genetic counsellor first.'

'You mean, so I might not have long QT?'

'Sorry, that's not what I meant. You do have long QT, love.'

'How do they know if I haven't even had the test?'

'Because they've measured your heart rhythms. The genetic test just confirms the diagnosis.'

'What's the point of it then?'

'Well, the genetic test will confirm which of your genes is affected and what type of long QT syndrome you have. Also, sometimes family members who don't have symptoms might still have a long QT gene, which they might want to know.'

'The whole thing is stupid,' I say.

'I am so sorry,' says Mum.

'Why are you sorry?' I say.

'It's my fault.' Mum's voice sounds wobbly.

'It's not your fault. It's that doctor's fault. There's nothing wrong with me. I can run fast for ages.'

'It's nobody's fault,' says Dad. 'This kind of heart disease isn't about how fit you are, it's about your genes and how your body is made.'

'Well, even if I do have it, you said long QT doesn't change who Mum is. So it shouldn't change who I am either. I'm not going to stop running.'

'You have to,' says Dad. I can tell he's getting

annoyed, and I'd normally stop arguing, but this is too important.

'But I never have any problems when I'm running. I don't faint all over the place like Mum.'

'Sometimes the first symptom of long QT is when the person goes into cardiac arrest. That could happen to you,' says Mum.

'*And*,' Dad joins in to gang up on me, 'you have fainted before. Twice. The doctor told us that fainting can be a warning of something more serious.' Dad is talking through gritted teeth, which he always does when he's angry but pretending to be calm and reasonable.

'That was different!' I'm talking loudly now, trying to get through to him. 'The first time I was just worried about the needle because Holly went on and on about it touching her arm bone. And the second time I hit my head on the side of the pool because I'm unco! You can't stop me from running. I'll go to Bundoora by myself!'

Dad raises his voice too. 'Vivian! You have to listen to the doctors.'

Mum puts her hand on Dad's. 'Calm down. Remember, we're supposed to stay calm!'

'I don't need to stay calm!' I shout and bang the car door with my fist. 'I can get as angry as I want, and look! I still haven't had a heart attack.'

I expect Dad to argue because he hates it when someone else has the last word, but he doesn't. Mum and Dad just become really quiet in the front seats of the car.

When we get home, I put on my running shorts, my singlet and shoes. I'm done with wasting time. Who knows how much training the other regional champions have been doing? I need to catch up.

I go to the front door and pass Dad coming in from the car.

'What are you doing?'

'Nothing.'

'Are you going for a run?'

I don't say anything as I slip past Dad and down the steps.

'Vivian!' he yells. 'Come back!'

I jog towards the gateway and run faster when I get onto the dirt road. I'm running towards the river. I sprint as fast as I can. I'm flying. I feel my heart beating in my chest sending the blood around my body. It is working perfectly. I am working perfectly.

I'm not going to have problems with my heart. If you believe you will succeed or believe you will fail, you're right. I believe in myself and believe in my body. I am fine. If you have a passion and you work hard enough, you can achieve anything. I have a passion and I will work harder than anyone. They can't stop me.

My legs ache but I ignore the pain. I run to the river then turn around and run back. I'd bet anything in the world that Dad and Noah can't run like me.

I arrive home sweaty, breathless, alive.

That night I'm so tired, I go to bed at eight o'clock. I wake up when it's still dark feeling very confused. I look at the time, and it's only eleven, not even the middle of the night. Mum and Dad are still up – I can hear them talking. Actually, they're arguing. I think that's what woke me.

'Why are you angry at me?' says Mum.

'I'm not.'

'You look angry, you sound angry. So logic tells me you're angry.'

'If I say I'm not angry, then I'm not angry,' yells Dad. 'All I'm saying is that if you hadn't waited so long, then maybe we wouldn't be in this situation now. You *knew* about Liam.'

'You knew too.'

'But it's not my family. It's not *me*.'

There's a long pause. Someone slams the dish-washer door shut.

'Anyway, you're the one who's always pushing the kids into sports,' Mum says.

'This is *my* fault now? Seriously? You want to make this my fault? I wanted her to have a healthy life.'

'She still can have a healthy life.'

'Really? Is it a healthy life if she has to worry about dropping dead every time she touches cold water or she walks too fast up a hill? Some life.'

'You. Are. Exaggerating.'

No one talks for a little while.

Later, I hear Mum crying and Dad apologising. They don't know that I heard them, but now I know how they really feel. I agree with Dad. If I can't run, my life is over.

14

DEBATING

Dad drives me to school the day after our visit to the doctor. Because he has me trapped in the car Dad talks on and on about how kids have died from long QT syndrome and that if I won't make adjustments, I might need to have a machine in my chest for the rest of my life. The machine gives you a shock if your heart isn't working properly and apparently it feels horrible. Dad says he knows it's disappointing for me, but I can still do lots of things and I should focus on those.

Only last night I heard Dad say, 'Some life.' I know what he really thinks. He won't say it to me, but he says it to Mum when he thinks I can't hear.

I don't see the point of being alive if I have to just sit around relaxing, but arguing with Dad is a waste of time, so I don't say anything. Dad hates that even more. He wants me to say that I agree with him, but I don't, so I won't.

I'm very happy to get out of the car. At the bottom of the hill, Olivia is waiting by the side of the road. 'Are you ready?' she asks.

'What for?'

'Olympic debating. Remember, today's our turn?'

I'd completely forgotten. Even though we've spent weeks working on our Olympic debates, I'm not ready. Luckily, there's no way the Olympics should be cancelled, so it won't be very hard for my team to win.

As per usual, Olivia is very well prepared. She's made speaking notes on a card, but she doesn't think she'll need them.

The debate isn't until the afternoon because Matt says the last time a class of his did a debate in the morning, they were overwrought for the rest of the day.

It's hard for me to concentrate on class work. I only get six out of ten in maths Quick Questions, and I get 'embarrassing' wrong in spelling.

At lunchtime the others want to play handball and I play with them. But I worry that I'm dizzy, so I say I need a drink of water. After I go to the bubbler, I sit on the bench.

I'm annoyed at myself because the doctor and my mum and dad have made me imagine bad things. Olivia's right – doctors do make you sick. If I'd never been tested for long QT syndrome, I would have been fine. Now I'm turning into the kind of person who needs to rest all the time.

After lunch it's time for the class debates. The other members of Team Spain, Liza and Calvin, are very excited. I just want to get it won and done.

Matt sets up six chairs at the front of the class, three on the left for Team USA and three on the right for Team Spain.

Holly stands at the front of the class to speak first for Team USA. She starts by defining the Olympics as the modern Summer Olympic Games, which were started in 1896 in Athens by a French man called Pierre de Coubertin, and the Winter Olympic Games, which began in 1924 in Chamonix, France. I don't think Chamonix should rhyme with Weet-Bix, but it does when Holly says it. She says that her team will demonstrate that the main people who benefit from the Olympic Games are corporations and evil governments, and therefore the world would be better off if the Olympics were cancelled.

What would Holly know? She hates sport. She doesn't understand that the Olympics inspire people and show human beings at their best.

Liza speaks first for our team. She says we need to expand the definition of the Olympics to include the Paralympics, which is a very good point.

Next up, Sam argues that the Olympics should be cancelled. He talks about the negative effects on the host cities, how homeless people get kicked out of Olympic areas, and that after the games are over, the Olympic buildings aren't useful for the people who live in the host cities. He says the Olympics are mainly about making money, and you can tell because they let countries who are really bad at human rights host the Olympics. Sam says the Olympics are used by evil governments to convince the world they are good. At the Berlin Olympics in 1936, Hitler was showing off the whole time, and by being there all the other countries were basically saying that Hitler was okay.

Then Sam says that the Olympics aren't even good for athletes because elite athletes wreck their bodies and take drugs. Most athletes don't make much money, and when they get too old, they don't have another career. He says that elite athletes are like gladiators, killing themselves for other people's entertainment.

That is so wrong. I shouldn't even have to say why. It is so obvious.

When I stand at the front of the class I'm shaking, partly because I'm nervous but also because I'm so mad about what Sam said. I can't believe I thought I knew him.

My brain freezes. I look down at the piece of paper in my hands and read: 'The opposition says that the Olympic Games are linked to countries doing bad things. This might be true, but it doesn't *cause* countries to do bad things. And having the world spotlight on them during the Olympics can make countries be better.

'If the Olympics were cancelled, the world would be a much worse place. The Olympics bring people joy, improve infrastructure and show how good humans can be. The Olympics should not be cancelled.'

That's the end of what I'd written, but it wasn't long enough because no one claps.

Calvin hisses, 'Health of athletes,' at me.

'Calvin, no coaching,' says Matt.

Oh yeah, I'm supposed to say something about Sam's argument about gladiators. 'Sam said that sport is bad for people,' I say. 'That's not true. It's not bad for athletes. Sport is good for people. It helps with diabetes and stops people being unhealthy.'

I can't think of anything else to say so I sit down. The class claps, but not as much as they did for the others. Liza leans over and says, 'Go, Team Spain!'

Olivia speaks next. She holds her speaking notes but doesn't even glance down at them. She knows exactly what she wants to say.

'I'm afraid,' she says, 'that Team Spain have entirely missed the point. We are not arguing that *sport in and of itself* is bad for people, but that the Olympics does nothing to promote sport in the broader community. Watching and doing are not the same things. Watching Kipchoge win a marathon on the television will do absolutely nothing to lower the blood sugar levels of a diabetic.'

Matt chuckles as if she's said something funny.

Olivia continues. 'Also, although participating in sport is definitely good for most of the population, it is equally true that high-level training is damaging to the health of Olympic athletes who participate in sport in an entirely different way.'

Olivia is actually trying to win the debate. I didn't expect this – she's supposed to be on my side. Just because she doesn't want to go to the Olympics anymore, doesn't mean she should ruin it for everyone else.

'Rather than improving their health outcomes, their participation in elite performance sport leads to' – Olivia quickly looks at her cards – 'chronic injuries, malnourishment and health problems later in life.'

Olivia sounds like someone from the television. She doesn't sound like my friend.

'Consider the famous example of the 1988 men's 100 metres final, where four of the top five athletes went on to have their careers tainted by drug scandals. Doping is now *the norm* in some Olympic sports and these events can't be viewed as fair competition in these circumstances.'

Speaking of fair competition, I think Olivia's dad helped her write this debate speech.

Olivia pauses, but not because she doesn't know what to say. She's just doing it to be dramatic. 'It's the prestige, money and power of the Olympics that cause these problems and lead athletes to sacrifice their bodies and health for glory and our entertainment,' she says eventually. 'I'm disappointed that Team Spain failed to grasp this essential point.'

I have heard enough. 'That's not true,' I say.

Matt waves at me to sit down. 'Team Spain will have another chance to rebut when Olivia's finished.'

I keep talking. 'You don't understand what the Olympics mean to people. Just because you gave up, doesn't mean everyone else should.'

Matt interrupts again. 'Vivian, you had your chance to speak.'

I sit down. Everyone in the class is staring at me, I can tell, even though I'm looking out the window.

'So, yes, the Olympics should be cancelled for the benefit of our communities, cities, and particularly, for the health of the athletes themselves,' Olivia finishes.

Calvin speaks last for our team and rebuts Team USA's arguments. He's good at talking and doesn't need to use notes, but I can't concentrate on what he's saying because I'm too angry at Olivia. She's just so wrong. Surely Matt will understand that when he judges the debate. Calvin talks for too long, and Matt rings the bell so Calvin has to stop before he finishes properly.

Matt says the quality of the debate was very high overall. 'I've added up the scores,' he says. 'The important thing to remember about debating is that it's not about which side is *correct* or who I may or may not agree with. It's about which side did the better job of making a convincing argument. It's also important that we don't take debating too personally. Both teams did a good job today, but the winner is the affirmative, Team USA, who argued that the Olympics *should* be cancelled.'

I can't believe this. It is so wrong.

Dad asks lots of questions in the car on the way home from school. I don't say much. I'm thinking about the debate and all of the things I should have said. When I was standing in front of the class, I couldn't put my arguments into words. Olivia had no problem with that. She had all the fancy words and the arguments, even if she was completely wrong. But, apparently, being wrong doesn't matter. And Sam was in on it too. He and Olivia are just the same. Maybe they like each other.

I go straight to my room when we arrive home, and I put on my runners and shorts. I head out the back door. Mum is putting on a load of washing in the laundry, but I slip past her.

'Remember to walk or jog at an easy pace,' she yells as I jump down the steps. 'Make sure you can still carry out a conversation!'

I walk to the gate and then I jog slowly for 100 metres until there are trees between me and the house.

Then I run. Every time I remember Olivia saying, 'The Olympics should be cancelled,' I run a little faster. After I've been running for a few minutes, I don't feel angry about the debate anymore. Instead, I'm embarrassed that I made a fool of myself. But I'm also sad for Olivia. She has changed so much. She's given up on her dreams and now she'll never achieve them. She believes she won't succeed, so she won't.

I run to the river and turn around and run back. I slow down to walk before I get to the house, so that Mum and Dad won't know I've been running.

When I walk in the gate, Noah is in the backyard taking the washing off the line, which is weird.

'Where have you been?' he asks me.

'I went for a walk.'

'Your face is all red.'

'No, it's not.'

'Have you been running?'

'Only at an easy pace. I was able to carry out a conversation the whole time.'

'Yeah, right.'

I don't care if Noah doesn't believe me. I walk past him towards the house.

'And don't bang the door,' he says.

'I'll bang the door if I want. You're not the boss of me.'

'Mum's asleep. She needs to rest.'

'Calm your farm, drama llama.'

I walk up the steps. Only five minutes after my run and Noah has completely ruined my mood. At the top of the steps I shut the door firmly, but it's not quite a bang. I hope that shows Noah that I could bang the door if I wanted.

Everyone is making such a fuss about long QT syndrome, but Mum and I are fine. Although Mum might not be as fine as me because she faints all the time.

In my room, I take off my shoes and socks. My socks are drenched with sweat. I sniff my feet. They don't smell good. Maybe I need foot deodorant before the state cross country final.

Through the window I see Noah trying to fold up a big doona cover from the washing line. He drags it on the ground. It will need to be washed again.

Noah is so annoying. Why does he care if I run? I never criticised him for giving up footy, even though he is probably setting himself up for a life of sedentary behaviour and associated health issues.

I walk into the backyard again. 'It's none of your business if I run,' I say to Noah.

'Yeah, sure – it's none of my business if you kill

yourself. I look forward to being an only child again.'

'I'm not going to kill myself. You said it yourself, I couldn't run as fast as I do if my heart wasn't okay.'

'That was before a *cardiologist* diagnosed you with a heart condition. I think he knows more about it than we do.'

'Well, there are risks in everything. You could get hit by a bus crossing the road. That doesn't mean you should never cross a road again.'

'Yeah, but you can cross the road at the lights, and you can look both ways before you cross. What you're doing is shutting your eyes and walking into the traffic pretending it will be okay if you think happy thoughts.'

'It's alright for you,' I say. 'Just because *you* quit sport. You don't care if you sit around all day every day. I *love* running. And I'm good at it. I was going to the state cross country final. What am I supposed to do, just give up?'

'Yes. You have to find something else to do. Something that won't kill you.'

'What's the point of being alive if you can't do what you love?'

'Life. That's the point.'

I think about what I heard Dad say. 'Some life,' I say.

'It's literally all you've got.'

'I don't care. I want to run.'

'Can you think about someone else for a change? Can you think about Mum? She already feels guilty and now you won't listen to the doctors. And she's sick too.'

'I care about Mum.'

'Well, don't act like a spoilt brat then.' Noah is still getting the washing off the line and he doesn't have to stand on tiptoes like I do. Maybe one day I'll start growing like Noah did.

'I'm nice to Mum,' I say.

'What have you done for her?' asks Noah, reaching up to unpeg the last towel. His shirt isn't long enough so I can see his stomach.

'What have *you* done?'

'I'm getting the washing in.' He gestures towards the pile of washing in the basket.

'For the first time *in your life.* And by the way, that's not where the pegs go.'

'I'm not stressing her out by trying to kill myself!' he yells.

'But you are!' I yell back, because I'm so worried and angry that I can't keep it in anymore. 'You are killing yourself! You never do any exercise and you're fat. That's just as bad!'

We're both silent. It's the first time I've called

Noah fat. It's the first time I've called anyone fat. Mum won't let anyone say that word in our house because bodies come in all shapes and sizes and we're all beautiful. But I read articles in Dad's *Athletics World* magazines about how being overweight is bad for your health and means you'll die younger, and I don't want that to happen to my brother.

For once, Noah isn't saying anything.

The screen door opens and Mum stands at the top of the steps.

'You're supposed to be having a rest,' says Noah.

'It's a little bit difficult. What's going on?'

'Vivian went for a run,' says Noah. 'A fast one. She was all sweaty and red.'

'Noah, don't inform on your sister,' says Mum. 'Please just take the washing inside.'

Noah picks up the basket and lugs it past me up the stairs. Mum walks down the steps. She sits beside me and says, 'Vivian,' like it's a full sentence.

'Mum.'

I cry and she hugs me.

'I'm so sorry this has happened to you,' she says.

'It's not your fault.'

'It's no one's fault, but I'm still sorry.'

'I thought you blamed Dad for making me love sport?'

'What?'

'I heard you arguing the other night.'

There's a long pause, then Mum says, 'Dad and I were upset. When something like this happens, everyone has a lot of feelings. We said things we didn't mean.'

'So you're not getting divorced?'

Mum laughs. 'No. I think we can put up with each other for a bit longer.'

That's something at least. I feel a little bit better, but then I remember what Noah said.

'I'm sorry I'm not nice to you,' I say.

'But you are.'

'I'm not,' I say. The tears pour out and onto the shoulder of her jumper. I bury my face and sob. Noah is right, I am selfish. Mum's sick too, but I'm the one crying. I should be looking after her.

'What am I going to be now?' I say when I can finally talk again.

'You'll be Vivian,' she says. 'You're still the same person.'

'But I want to be an athlete.'

'I know.'

Mum and I sit on the steps together and I rest my head on her shoulder. I've stopped crying, but every so often a shuddery breath shows that I've only just stopped, and I might start again.

15

SICK

The next day, I don't get out of bed. Even when I hear the seven o'clock news bulletin on the radio, I stay in bed. Even when Dad yells, 'Ten-minute warning!', I stay in bed. Even when Mum yells, 'Vivian! We're leaving!', I don't move.

Mum comes barging into my room. 'Vivian! Why are you still in bed!'

'I feel sick.'

'What kind of sick?'

'Flu sick.'

Mum rests her hand on my forehead. She asks me to open my mouth. She checks my stomach for a rash. 'You seem fine.'

'You're not a doctor.'

'Vivian.'

I sit up and swing my legs out of the bed. 'Okay, I'm coming.'

I get dressed and go to the kitchen. The breakfast things have been put away, so I get the Weet-Bix out again.

'We don't have time for that,' says Mum. 'You can have a breakfast drink.' She hands me a carton from the fridge.

'Dad says these are basically just sugar.'

'I know.'

'Why did you buy them then?'

'Because I'm very busy and important. You can drink it in the car.'

I go to the bathroom and brush my teeth. When I get out, Mum is holding my schoolbag for me.

Dad points at the breakfast drink I'm holding. 'I thought we discussed those?'

'Don't start,' says Mum. He already has, but he stops.

In the car, I poke the straw into the breakfast drink and take a sip. It tastes disgusting, although to be fair, so do most things straight after you brush your teeth.

Olivia is still waiting for me at the bottom of the hill, even though I'm late. I shove the drink carton into the compartment on the car door. I don't want Olivia to catch me with it. It would be worse than when Holly brought Fruit Roll-Ups to school and said they were as healthy as eating a piece of fruit.

'You're late,' says Olivia as I get out of the car.

'I overslept.'

'Are you still upset about the debate?'

'I was never upset.'

'You seemed upset.'

'I don't even care about the debate.'

We can hear the song playing. It's the one about growing up again. It's a very sad song.

Faye is standing at the gate when Olivia and I walk in, and she asks to speak to me in her office. I follow her across the basketball court to the office block. I hope I'm not in trouble for poor debatepersonship.

But when we get there it's not just Matt in her office. Alex, Mum and Dad are also sitting in chairs opposite Faye's desk. So much for Mum needing to go to work early. More like needing to gang up on me with the other teachers.

'Vivian, have a seat,' says Faye, pointing to the empty chair next to Mum.

I sit down.

'Your mum told us about your diagnosis with long QT syndrome,' says Faye. 'That must be very hard.'

'It's okay,' I say, because I don't want to talk to teachers about it.

'I understand that you won't be able to compete in the state cross country final.'

Faye and Alex both love sport. Maybe this could be a chance to get someone else on my side.

'I could still do it,' I say. 'I haven't even had the genetic test yet, so maybe it's a mistake. Also, I've been for a couple of runs and I was fine.'

'That's not an option,' says Mum.

'It is! Just this one race. Just let me do this one last race.' I look at Alex and then at Faye. 'I swear, I feel fine. I could tell you if I ever felt funny.'

'But that's the problem,' says Mum. 'You would probably feel completely normal until it happened. There often aren't warning signs.'

'I'm afraid the school won't be able to enter you in the race,' says Faye.

'Why not! I earned it. I won the regional final.'

'You don't have your parents' permission.'

'I'm sorry,' says Dad. 'We've explained to Vivian what her limitations are, but it's difficult.'

'We wanted to talk to you about a plan for how you can participate in sports activities at school,' says Faye in a cheerful voice. 'We want to help you by focussing on what you *can* do.'

It's easy for her to feel happy about it – no one is

taking away her dream.

I can't convince them to give me a chance, so I give in and stop talking.

I'm not interested in what anyone has to say, but Mum, Dad, Faye and Alex have a good old chat about me. I expected Alex to stick up for me, but he is on their side. He asks lots of questions about what activities are appropriate and writes notes on a piece of paper. He doesn't even seem disappointed. I guess I wasn't special after all. Saying I had *a bit of ability* didn't mean much in the end.

Matt is looking very serious and nodding a lot. I don't know why he's even here because he never does sport with us. He hates sports, which is probably why he was against me in the Olympics debate.

Faye says the school is getting a defibrillator machine, which can start people's hearts if they have a heart attack. It's a total waste of money – they should buy something good, like a proper starter's pistol. Mum and Dad have ordered a defibrillator for our house too. It's very expensive, so I guess Noah won't get a new trumpet this year. I think everyone should prioritise better.

Faye says we should talk about new interests for me.

I am not interested in new interests. Some kids change what they want to do every week. I've heard Nasrin say that she wants to be an actor, an archaeologist and a lawyer, and that's just this year. The only thing I've wanted for the past four years is to go to the Olympics, and now I can't. Unlike Faye, I don't think joining a ten-pin bowling team could be a good option to explore because ten-pin bowling is not an Olympic sport. Matt actually suggests chess. Seriously.

'Are you okay, Vivian?' asks Faye.

'I'm fine,' I say. I really am fine. I wish they would believe me.

Mum, Dad, Matt and Alex stand up. Mum and Dad keep thanking Faye as we leave her office. She says goodbye to me in her usual cheerful voice. She doesn't get it.

Back in the grade five portable Olivia asks, 'What did they want?'

'Just about Mum being sick,' I say as I sit down.

I don't want Olivia to think that I've given up at the first hurdle like she did.

Liza and I work in a pair in maths. We have to spin a spinner and write down which colour it lands on. The blue triangle is much smaller than all the others, but I am barracking for that one.

I spin the arrow. 'Green again,' I say, and Liza puts a mark in the green column.

'I have something for you,' says Liza. She feels in her tracksuit pants pocket and pulls out a lump of rock. 'It's an agate crystal,' she says. 'You know how I told you rocks have healing powers?'

I remember, but I didn't believe her.

'Well, this one's good for your heart. You could give it to your mum.'

'Thanks.' I look at the crystal, which has one polished smooth surface with coloured rings in red, yellow and pink.

'Are you sure? It looks expensive.'

'That's okay. You can't put a price on health. Only, don't tell Olivia.'

'Why not?'

'She can be a bit judgemental about alternative medicines.'

I don't want Liza to think I'm judging her like Olivia, so I put the crystal in my pencil case to take home. I don't think Mum should put it under her pillow, though. It might give her a cricked neck.

When I get home that afternoon, I go to my room to put my bag away. I take out the agate crystal and put it on my bookshelf. I like looking at it. It makes me feel calm, even if I don't believe it has healing powers.

*

The next day we have sport with Alex first thing. We're having a soccer game, not skills exercises like last week. Alex asks me to umpire.

'No thanks,' I say.

'I think it would be a good idea,' he says.

'No, I want to play.'

'I need to talk to you for a moment.' Alex motions for me to come and stand with him a little apart from the rest of the class.

'You know soccer is on the list, Vivian,' says Alex. 'You can participate in the exercises, but I can't risk having you play in the game.'

'But I won't get hurt. I'll be careful.'

'You'll be careful. It's the other kids I'm worried about.'

I bet he's thinking of Daniel. Sometimes he deliberately trips people over. And Liza sometimes knocks people over, not on purpose, but once she's playing, the only thing she sees is the ball.

'What am I supposed to do then?'

'You can be the umpire,' says Alex.

'Alright,' I say, only because I have just thought of something. Dad once told me that AFL umpires are great runners so they can keep up with the game. People don't realise how fit they are. Umpiring could be a chance for me to run without anyone noticing.

‘Good girl. That’s the spirit.’

Alex gives me an orange vest and a whistle. I can’t remember the rules of soccer except that you can’t touch the ball with your hands, but Alex says he’ll stick with me and tell me what to do.

The game starts, and I jog up and down and follow the ball around the oval from a safe distance. Alex does the actual umpiring, saying when someone breaks a rule and bossing everyone around. He blows his whistle a lot.

The two teams are very evenly matched. Most people don’t know what they’re doing, so about ten people run after the ball and then they all get stuck in a bunch kicking each other’s shins. I’m not really sorry that I can’t play. Alex keeps yelling at people to spread out, and Daniel and Liza get frustrated because they’re the only people who have any skills or clue.

Everyone forgets about me, so I do mini-sprints from one set of goalposts to the other. I look at my watch and try to do each sprint faster than the last one. I rest for one minute between each one.

I’m on my fifth sprint when I hear Alex’s whistle blowing furiously. At first, I assume it’s for the soccer game, but then I hear him yell, ‘Vivian! Stop!’

I slow down and turn around. The whole class stares as Alex walks towards me.

'What are you doing?' he says.

'Umpiring,' I say.

Alex says I have to sit on the bench for the rest of the class.

At recess, the three of us sit around our table.

'So, what was that about?' Olivia asks.

'Yeah, why was Alex so mean to you?' Liza adds.

'He wasn't mean,' I say.

'Yes, he was,' says Olivia. 'First, he wouldn't let you play and made you be umpire. Then he made you sit on the bench. It was unfair.'

I shrug.

'Is it because of your mum?'

'Is it for training?'

'Is Alex having mental health issues like Brendan?'

'Is Alex secretly in love with you?'

'Are you both in a gang together and you robbed a bank and now you won't tell Alex where you've hidden the cash?'

We all laugh. But they're still waiting for an answer.

'The doctors think I've got long QT syndrome,' I say. 'The same thing my mum has, that makes her heart go funny. Mum and Dad and all the teachers are being annoying about it.'

No one's laughing and coming up with theories anymore. No one says anything.

The song plays, so I stand up and walk towards the grade five portable. Olivia runs up beside me. 'You can't do that,' she says.

'Do what?'

'Drop a bomb like that and then just walk off.'

'It's not a bomb. I don't even think it's true.'

I walk up the ramp to the portable and over to my locker. I get out my zippers pencil case and my ruler for maths.

We're doing our first worksheet when Olivia whispers, 'Do you have to take medicine?'

'I dunno. Probably.'

I look at my worksheet. I'm finding it very difficult to concentrate on the chance of rolling a seven with two dice. Olivia shows me the answer. Normally she says she'll explain things to me, but she usually won't give the answers because I won't learn anything that way. She gets that from her dad because he's a maths teacher.

I write '1/6' on my worksheet. Sometimes it's useful when people feel sorry for you.

The next question is just as bad. It's the chance of rolling a two.

Faye comes into the classroom and whispers to Matt. Then I have to go with her to her office.

I shrug at Olivia pretending I don't know what it's about.

Of course, Alex and Dad are waiting in Faye's office. Faye says we need to talk about what happened during the soccer game.

'Nothing happened.'

'Your parents haven't given you permission to participate in games,' says Faye. 'Because of your condition.'

'I wasn't participating in the game.'

'What were you doing then?'

'Jogging.'

'You weren't jogging,' says Alex. 'You were sprinting flat out.'

'I was not.'

'Well, you must be the best runner in the world,' says Alex. 'You're good, but you're not that good. You were running sprint intervals between the goalposts. I gave you the benefit of the doubt at first, but then you ran faster and faster. I'm responsible for you in PE class. I'm the one people will blame. So you need to pull your head in.'

'I don't want to just give up,' I say. 'I want to go to the state final.'

'You can't,' says Dad.

'Why not? It's just one more race.'

'There will always be one more race,' says Alex.

'What happens if you do well in the state final and you get into the nationals?'

The national final. I hadn't even thought of that.

'Do you think I would?'

'It's possible,' says Alex.

Dad interrupts. 'But that's not the point, Vivian. You need to accept your limitations.'

Alex agrees. 'Yes, that's right.'

'Just because you didn't go to the Commonwealth Games, Alex, doesn't mean everyone else should give up like you did.'

There. I've said it.

'I didn't just give up,' says Alex after a pause. 'I stuffed my knees when I was playing footy and I couldn't run anymore.'

'You could have had an operation.'

'I couldn't. Sometimes it's not about how hard you try.'

That's not what I've heard. What's the point of the school getting Susie Maroney to speak to us if everyone ignores what she said? I don't remember Susie saying, 'Accept your limitations' in her motivational speech. She said, 'You can do *anything* if you work hard enough.' My only limitation is that everyone wants to stop me.

The bell rings for lunch. I look at Faye. 'Can I go?'

'Yes,' she says. 'But please, Vivian, follow Alex's

instructions or you'll have to go to the library during PE, and no one wants that.'

At lunchtime, the only thing Liza wants to talk about is long QT syndrome. It's almost like she's excited about it. I tell her and Olivia I'm not supposed to run fast or do rough sports.

'Can they fix long QT syndrome?' asks Liza.

'They don't think so.'

'My dad once went to a heart specialist in Melbourne,' says Liza. 'You could see him.'

'I've seen a heart specialist in Bendigo.'

'What about giving up gluten?' says Liza.

'How would that help?'

'It's supposed to help with lots of things.'

'I don't think it will help with this.'

'You have to stay positive,' says Liza. 'Try everything. You never know.'

'Well, the specialist doctor will write a treatment plan for me.'

'So will that fix it?'

'I don't know. I think the treatment plan is just rules and tests and medication.'

'So there *is* medication?' says Liza.

'Yeah.'

'Well, that's okay then.'

'The medication can't cure the long QT

syndrome. It just makes it less likely that I'll have a heart attack.'

Liza shuts up for a few moments. Then she says, 'What about a heart transplant?'

I stand up. 'I'm going to the library.'

I go to the spot between the non-fiction shelves in front of the sports books. It used to be my favourite section of the library. I move up until I'm opposite the space books.

Someone sits beside me. It's Olivia. She doesn't say anything and we both just sit there. I can't stand the awkward silence so I randomly pick up a book off the shelf. It's about stars. I pretend to read it for a few minutes.

'Liza doesn't get it,' Olivia finally says.

I close the book and stop pretending to read. 'She thinks it's my fault for not trying hard enough. Maybe she's right.'

'It's not your fault.'

'How do you know?'

'I did some research on long QT.'

'What kind of research?'

'I googled it.'

I sigh. 'I know it sounds really bad. And all the adults are really worried.' I pick at bits of fluff on the carpet and start to make a little pile. 'But I just want to go to the state cross country final.'

Olivia doesn't reply. The old Olivia would have come up with a plan to get me there. She wouldn't let me give up on my dream. Eventually Olivia says, 'I'm going to cure it.'

'What?'

'Long QT syndrome. When I grow up, I'm going to become a doctor and find a cure.'

'It will take you twenty years to become a proper doctor. And you have to become a specialist doctor, and that takes even longer.'

'It doesn't matter how long it takes – I'm going to do it.'

'It won't help me. I'll be, like, forty by then. I won't be able to run fast anyway.'

'I know. I'm sorry about that. But maybe I can fix it for the next generation.'

I believe her. When Olivia is determined, she doesn't give up. Except on her Olympic dreams, but it seems like everyone in the world does that.

16

CURE

Olivia is excited when I meet her at the bottom of the hill on Monday. 'I have news!' she says. 'I've been researching.'

'Researching what?'

'Long QT syndrome. There was a swimmer in America called Dana Vollmer. She had long QT syndrome. But she kept training and she went to the London Olympic Games and won a gold medal!'

'Are you joking?'

'No, it's true.'

'But then why would my parents and the doctors say I can't run?'

We walk the rest of the way up the hill in silence. I have a lot to think about. Maybe the doctor isn't as good as everyone thinks. Maybe he's not world-class. Maybe he doesn't know everything. Maybe I need a second opinion. Maybe, there's hope.

Dad picks me up after school. In the car on the way home he tells me about his day. He's designing a new website for a community radio station. 'You're looking for a new hobby, aren't you?' he says.

'No.'

'Well, you are, because you can't do your running anymore.'

'I guess so,' I say. I won't tell Dad about Dana Vollmer yet. I'll wait until I've done my own research. Then he won't be able to win the argument because I will know more than him.

'Radio 3PT are looking for cadet presenters, ages ten to sixteen.'

'What even is a cadet?'

'They'll teach you about how to present on radio and what all the buttons and knobs do.'

'That sounds boring.'

'It could be fun. I thought you really liked *The Sports Report* on Radio 3PT.'

Dad doesn't understand me. I *used* to like that show.

'You could at least put in an application. No harm in that.'

I don't say anything.

When we get home, Dad shows me the online application form for the Radio 3PT cadetship. Maybe it would be kind of fun to be on radio and have my voice coming into people's cars and lounge rooms and shops. People like Sam might even listen to me. And I could wear headphones and talk into the microphone.

On the other hand, sitting around talking is totally boring compared to running.

I agree to fill in the application, mainly so Dad will stop going on about it.

The first part of the form is easy because I know my own name and address. The second part has hard questions about why I want to be a cadet, what I would bring to Radio 3PT and what community radio means to me.

I have a go at writing the answers. Dad reads them and says you're not supposed to be that honest in an application. He makes suggestions. I thought you weren't supposed to lie, but Dad says you're expected to exaggerate a little bit in a job application. I'm not sure that saying I have a passion for something I've never even thought about before counts as exaggerating, but I can't be bothered arguing.

I click submit.

Dad says we need more irons in the fire, so we also look up pottery classes, acting courses, singing lessons, and something called callisthenics that we'll have to ask the doctor about because it might be too strenuous.

'You see,' says Dad. 'There's more to life than running.'

Some life, I think, and I know that deep down Dad agrees with me.

When Dad finally leaves me alone with the computer, I look up Dana Vollmer.

Everything Olivia said about her is true.

Then I wonder if there are other athletes who have long QT. I find an article about a study of athletes with the syndrome. One hundred and thirty athletes kept competing after being diagnosed with long QT, and only one of them had a cardiac arrest while competing – and that person didn't even die. That is what a scientific study says. You can't argue with science.

On Tuesday after school, I go back to the cardiologist with Mum and Dad to discuss my treatment plan.

But I have another plan. I'm going to tell them I know about Dana Vollmer. I've printed articles and made a list of my main points, in case I get nervous and forget my arguments, like in the class debate.

Doctor Stanford smiles a lot as we walk into the room. He says, 'How was school today, Vivian?' in a cheery voice.

'It was fine, thanks,' I say. 'We made masks in art.'

We sit down and Doctor Stanford starts talking about beta-blockers and tests. He hands Mum and Dad a folder with papers in it for them to read. Mum asks questions because she's become an expert on long QT medication since she got diagnosed.

Mum still doesn't have the results from her genetic test. Apparently, it will be up to me whether I want to be tested or not.

Dad asks, 'So just to clarify for Vivian, the genetic tests can confirm long QT, but you don't need it to make your diagnosis?'

'That's right,' Doctor Stanford says.

'So she does have long QT syndrome?'

'In my opinion, yes.'

Dad looks at me. 'Did you hear that, Vivian?'

'Yep.' Alright, alright, Dad.

'What about physical activity?' asks Mum.

'As discussed at your previous visit. No competitive rough sports or activities that excessively elevate the heart rate.'

It's now or never. I *have* to say something. 'What about Dana Vollmer?'

Doctor Stanford turns to me for the first time since we came in. 'What have you read about Dana Vollmer?'

'She was an Olympic athlete. She won a gold medal at the London Olympics and set a record *and* she had long QT syndrome.'

'Yes, that's largely accurate,' says Doctor Stanford.

'So you know about her?'

'Of course.'

'Then why do I have to give up running?'

Doctor Stanford goes into a long speech about how my condition is different to Dana Vollmer's. I've had different symptoms and a family history, and perhaps Dana Vollmer didn't really have long QT syndrome after all.

I'm not going to give up so easily in this debate. 'But haven't there been some studies where people with long QT didn't give up sport and they were fine?'

'Yes, but in those cases, the athletes had established an effective medication regime and had other precautions in place.'

I look back down at the piece of paper on my lap. 'But aren't there health risks in giving up sport as well?' I say. 'What about obesity and diabetes?'

'In my view, moderate exercise can counter those risks.'

I look down at my notes again. 'What about the risk of depression?'

'Counselling can help you with psychological issues.'

I've run out of notes and I still haven't won. 'What if I think there's no point being alive if I can't run?'

'Vivian!' says Dad, while Mum makes her funny gasping noise again.

Doctor Stanford waves his hand at them. 'Have you had many thoughts like that?' he asks me.

'No,' I say. 'But I can't see what the point of life is now. You know what I mean, don't you, Dad?'

'No, I don't,' Dad says in a wobbly voice. 'I really, really don't. You have so much to live for.'

'But I heard you saying that I wouldn't have a life. You said, "Some life."'

'That was the first day you were diagnosed,' he says. Dad wipes his cheek. I don't know why he's crying. He's not the one whose life is over. 'I was upset and I didn't know what I was saying. You have lots to live for.'

'This is a serious concern,' says Doctor Stanford. 'We need to take Vivian's mental health into account in her treatment plan.'

Doctor Stanford says that once the medication is working, we could modify the plan so I can participate in games, as long as there's a defibrillator nearby.

'And running?' I ask.

'In my opinion, you should not run competitively.'

'But why? If it's the only thing I care about?'

'You're ten years old,' says Mum. 'You might think you don't care about anything else, but if you live long enough you might change your mind.' Mum tries to put her arm around me, but I move away. Mum puts her hands back in her lap.

'I would recommend Vivian sees a psychologist to help her deal with the changes in her life,' Doctor Stanford says. 'I can give you a referral and I'll have my office call ahead to make sure an appointment is available for Vivian.'

So that's it. No state cross country final. I've lost before the race even starts.

We pick up my prescription from the chemist after leaving Doctor Stanford's office. I'm supposed to take one tablet every morning, maybe for the rest of my life. They might make me feel like I have less energy. I might also have nightmares, feel cold or dizzy, and about a thousand other problems I don't have now.

Dad brings the car around to the front of the

chemist to pick up Mum and me because it's raining.

I look out the car window at the drops of rain running down the glass. Until today I had hope that the doctor would change his mind, but now the treatment plan is set in stone. I lost.

Mum and Dad won't let me go to the state cross country final. I can't go to Melbourne by myself. I could catch a train and get off at Southern Cross Station. But I have no idea how to get to Bundoora. Also, I can't get to Bendigo train station in the first place.

I will never go to the Olympics.

Dad turns on the car radio. He changes the channel to Radio 3PT, the community station. *The Sports Report* is on but I don't want to hear about other people playing sport right now, even if they are really bad at it.

Matt marks the roll on Wednesday morning, then everyone starts heading outside for sport with Alex. I stay in my seat. Olivia and Liza stop at my desk. 'Are you coming?' Olivia asks.

'No,' I say.

Olivia looks confused. She looks over at Matt, who says, 'You go ahead, girls. I'll be here with Vivian.'

Olivia and Liza walk out of the classroom together. They're happy because they can go and play sport and be normal. I bet they won't even think about me.

'Why aren't you going to PE?' Matt asks.

'I'm not allowed, remember?'

'You're not allowed to do some activities, but there are plenty of things you can do.'

'Just the boring things.'

'So you're just going to sit in the classroom with me?'

'Yes.'

'Well, that sounds very boring. I'll be marking maths projects.'

Matt doesn't give me any work to do, so I just sit at my desk. I look around the room. I notice the spot on the carpet where Holly once vomited that will never be quite the same colour again. I look at our class self-portraits on the wall. Daniel drew himself without a mouth. A narrow beam of sunlight falls across my desk. I put my hands in the sunlight and feel them warming up.

I listen for my class playing and having fun outside without me, but all I can hear is the grade sixes next door, who seem to be moving all the chairs and tables around.

Matt is quiet at first but then he mutters little

comments to himself. Perhaps he's forgotten I'm here.

'Those probabilities add up to two,' he says. 'Interesting work.' I can tell he's being sarcastic.

I hope he's not looking at Liza's and my project. I stand up a little in my seat so I can see the poster and it's not ours, luckily.

The beam of light falling on my table is becoming wider. I put my head down on my arms and feel the warmth on my cheek. I could almost go to sleep like this.

'Vivian,' says Matt.

I don't answer straight away. I'm sleepy, and anyway Matt's not really the boss of me because I'm supposed to be in sport right now.

'Vivian,' he says, this time a little more loudly. Then he's in front of me shaking my shoulders.

'What?' I say, lifting up my head.

'Don't do that,' Matt says.

'What?'

'Not answer me.'

'I was just having a rest.'

Matt takes a deep breath. 'Right, well, I was just going to give you back your project since you're here.'

He hands me the poster that Liza and I worked on. We got ten out of ten and he's drawn a smiley face in the corner.

'It was really good work,' he says.

'Thanks.'

He turns to go back to his desk.

'Matt,' I say. 'You know the blue triangle?'

He nods.

'You know how we worked out the probability of a spin landing on a blue triangle was ten per cent?'

'Yep,' he says.

'And Liza and I did twenty spins and never got even one blue triangle?'

'Yep, that can happen.'

'Well, I think the probability of me having a heart attack is even less than that.'

'I'm not an expert on heart conditions,' says Matt. 'But your mum told me that long QT syndrome can be very serious.'

'But not everyone who has it dies. I could easily be one of the lucky ones.'

'I don't think we should be talking about this,' says Matt.

He goes back to his desk and looks at the next project, but he's a bit like my dad and he likes to have the last word. He can't resist saying one more thing. 'A ten per cent chance of landing on a blue triangle is one thing, but a ten per cent chance of dying is completely different. When it's real life, you need to look at the consequences, not just the probabilities.'

You should look at the rewards too, but I am done arguing with Matt. I put my head back on the desk. 'Don't worry,' I say to Matt. 'I'm not dead.'

17

MARATHON

At the end of the day, I step out of the portable and see Nana standing on the basketball court. 'Where's Dad?' I ask. Nana's visits are usually planned in advance because she has a lot of commitments. It's not normal for her to turn up out of the blue like this.

'I'm picking you up today,' says Nana, avoiding the question and stating the obvious.

I follow her to the car. Once I've shut the door, I ask the question again because I'm really worried now. 'Nana, where's Dad?'

Nana turns around in the front seat to look at me. 'I'm afraid your mum's not well. She's at the hospital and your dad's with her.'

'Did she have a heart attack?'

'No, but they're running some tests. I haven't got all the information yet, I'm sorry.'

'Are we going to the hospital now?'

'No, she can't have visitors at the moment.'

'But I want to see her.'

'That's not possible, Vivian.'

Nana turns on the car. She is done arguing.

We pick up Noah as well, and Nana gives him the same tiny amount of information. He gets really mad at her for not telling us more.

She grips the steering wheel and says firmly, 'I don't have anything to tell!'

I am so worried I feel sick.

At home, Nana opens a packet of Tim Tams.

I go back to my room. I'm surprised I'm not crying, that instead of being upset I mainly feel numb. I take the healing crystal off my bookshelf and look at it. Liza gave it to me for my mum, but I kept it for myself.

Nana lets me watch television for the rest of the day. I even eat dinner in front of the TV. I'm feeling very sleepy by ten o'clock, but I don't want to go to bed.

The next morning, I wake up in my bed and remember something isn't right. Mum's in hospital.

There's a tap on the door, followed by Nana's voice. 'Vivian. Time to get up.'

I find Nana making tea in the kitchen. 'Where's Dad?' I ask.

'He's gone back to the hospital,' says Nana. 'You were asleep when he came home last night. He put you to bed.'

I don't remember that at all.

Noah comes into the kitchen too, and Nana tells us what she knows about Mum. She has to stay in hospital for a while because she's having arrhythmias, which is when your heart doesn't beat regularly.

'I thought the medicine was supposed to help with that?' I say as I get out the Weet-Bix and a bowl.

'Sometimes medicine doesn't work straight away,' says Nana. 'Doctors aren't magicians, you know.'

I have more questions, but it doesn't seem like Nana will answer them.

Noah gets Weet-Bix for himself. Because Dad isn't here, he sprinkles two tablespoons of Milo on his cereal. I want to say something about it, but then I remember that I'm the one who ate five Tim Tams yesterday afternoon, so I don't.

*

Nana drives me to school. I don't think it's fair that I have to go to school today. How am I supposed to concentrate when Mum is in hospital?

Nana pulls up at the bottom of the hill to let me out.

Olivia comes over to the car holding a huge basket of fruit covered in plastic with flowers wound around the handle. 'It's from my mum for your mum,' she says. 'We heard she's in hospital.'

'That's very kind of you, Olivia,' says Nana.

Olivia opens the back door of the car and places the fruit on the back seat.

At least I know I can visit Mum today.

When school finishes, no one is there to pick me up. I have to go to the toilet and when I come back Olivia and Liza are playing handball against the wall. When she sees me, Olivia quickly catches the ball and puts it in her pocket.

Nana's car pulls up near the school gate.

'Say hi to your mum!' yells Olivia as I walk away.

Noah's in the front seat, so I get in the back. Nana's car is full of stuff, so I have to sit with Mum's fruit basket from Olivia on my knee.

As we pull away from the school, Liza and Olivia are playing handball again. There's no way they will spend the rest of grade five sitting in the library with me. They will go back to sport and I'll be alone.

'How was your day?' asks Nana.

'Fine. How's Mum?' I ask.

'She's doing really well. She's been very lucky, apparently.'

At the hospital we walk past the gift shop. I want to get Mum one of the silver helium balloons like Olivia got for me when I was in hospital. I ask Nana, but she says those balloons are a rip-off. 'It's not going to be a party in there, you know,' she says.

As if anyone thought that.

We take the lift to the third floor and Nana asks a nurse for directions.

Walking down the corridor, I peek into the other rooms. The patients are sleeping, watching television or doing puzzles. No one is being resuscitated or anything interesting.

Nana stops and pokes her head into a room. She waves for us to follow her. I walk in slowly, not sure what I'll see.

Mum is sitting up in bed. She's wearing a white gown and she has wires on her chest and arms that are attached to a machine. It's probably monitoring her heart.

'I brought you this,' I say, handing her the basket of fruit.

'That's so lovely!' says Mum. 'And very thoughtful!'

'Actually, it's from Olivia's mum.'

'Fenny is so nice. Shall we get started on it?' says Mum. She tries to take off the plastic but can't manage it. Nana takes out her car keys and stabs a hole in it.

Mum takes a mandarin. 'Do you want something?' she asks.

'It's supposed to all be for you,' I say.

'I can share.'

I take an apple and have a bite. I know it's normal fruit from the Fruit Mart, but it tastes better coming from a basket. Nana puts the basket on the floor next to Mum's bed. We will have to deal with the pawpaw later.

'I'm sorry about all this,' says Mum.

'Why are you sorry?' says Nana. 'It's not your fault you're sick.'

'But I was doing too much,' says Mum. 'I wanted to get the budget finalised.'

'You're going to have to let go of some things,' says Nana. 'I told you I can help more.'

'I know.'

'You can't do it all,' says Nana. 'You have to delegate.'

Mum nods.

'What actually happened?' I ask.

'I was at work,' says Mum. 'And the lift was being really slow, and I needed to talk to Rod by five, so I ran up the stairs. Just before I got to the top, I felt really funny and I fell backwards.'

'That's so dangerous!' I say. 'You've been told to take it easy!'

Noah coughs into his hand, but he actually says, 'Hypocrite.'

I am not a hypocrite. Mum is much sicker than I am. And anyway, it's heaps easier to give up doing boring budgets than your Olympic dream.

'Shut up, Noah,' I say.

'Shut up, Vivian,' Noah says.

'If you can't be good for your mother, I will take you both home,' says Nana.

'Mum, let's not be too hard on them.' My mum is trying to stick up for us because everyone knows Nana can be a grump.

'Okay. Fine,' says Nana. 'I'm going to get a coffee.'

She walks out of the room.

'When can you come home?' I ask Mum.

'Yeah,' says Noah. 'Nana's being a total grump.'

'This is very difficult for everyone,' says Mum. 'Do you want to help me fill this in?' She hands me a little piece of paper with the meal choices for the next day.

I use the little pencil and tick broccoli soup but also the ice-cream for balance. Nothing has goji berries, unfortunately. I guess it's because the government hardly gives public hospitals enough money for beds let alone official superfoods.

A nurse comes in and needs to do some observations, so Noah and I go into the corridor to wait. We sit in chairs against the wall and Noah takes out his phone. I don't have a phone, so I just sit and stare at the wall.

'I'm going to find a toilet,' I tell Noah, who doesn't even look up.

I walk down the corridor, past the nurses' desk, and turn the corner. I go over to the vending machine to check if anyone has accidentally left money. I reach in to the change compartment and pull out a coin. It's two dollars! I've been checking vending machines for years and have never found any money. Then I notice a lady sitting in a chair next to the machine. She has her head in her hands and she's crying.

It's my nana.

She looks up and sees me.

'Hi,' I say.

'Hi,' she says, wiping her eyes. 'Sorry, Vivian.'

'What's wrong?' I ask. Even though I suppose it's obvious. We were rude to her.

Nana smiles. 'Nothing's wrong, really. I'm so glad your mum's okay.'

'So why are you crying?'

'Well, I suppose I'm thinking about people who aren't okay.' Nana takes out a tissue and blows her nose.

'You mean Uncle Liam?'

Nana nods.

'Did he have long QT syndrome?'

'We don't know for sure. You know, he just collapsed at football training. They tried to revive him, but they couldn't do anything. They said it was sudden unexplained cardiac arrest. That was it.'

'That's so sad,' I say. The only thing Nana usually says about Liam is that he won lots of trophies and might have played for the AFL. I knew it was sad that he died, but I thought maybe she didn't think about it anymore.

'It's almost twenty-four years ago that he died,' Nana says. 'And seeing your mum today, I'm so relieved that she's okay, and that you're going to be safe, but I worry. And it reminds me. I still miss my boy.'

I feel helpless because I don't know what to say to make her feel better.

I remember my lucky two dollars, and I go back to the vending machine. I buy a KitKat and share it with Nana. I sit beside her chair on the floor and eat my two sticks.

Liam would be forty years old if he was still alive. If he had played for the AFL, his football career would be over, but he wouldn't be. I would have an uncle, Mum would have a brother, and Nana wouldn't be crying even when she's eating chocolate.

On Sunday morning, Mum is finally coming home. Dad goes to the hospital to pick her up, so Noah and I are in charge of making the house nice under Nana's supervision.

Noah vacuums the lounge room and I hang the washing out. Nana suggests we change the sheets on Mum and Dad's bed because it's lovely to come home to fresh clean sheets.

I take the pillowcases off while Noah strips the doona and sheets. I look in the linen cupboard and choose a green doona with dandelions because I read somewhere that natural themes are healing and restful. Noah and I pull opposite sides of the fitted sheet across the bed.

'Hey, Noah?' I say.

'What?'

'I'm sorry about the other day.'

'Which day?'

'When we had a fight. I called you something.'

'You mean you called me fat?'

'Yeah.'

'Don't worry about it.'

'But it was a mean thing to say.'

'Do you think it's the first time I've been called that?' Noah grabs one of the pillows and stuffs it into a pillowcase.

I get the doona cover and spread it across the bed. 'Who calls you fat?'

'Heaps of people. Not just fat. Jelly belly, lard arse, fatso, Noah the ark, the hippo.'

'That's so awful. Do they say that at school?'

Noah shrugs. 'Sometimes. I hate people looking at me. I hate getting changed in the locker rooms.'

'Quitting football won't help, though.'

'I don't care. I'm over it.'

'It's so unfair. I would give anything to play sport, but I'm not allowed. You can do anything you want, and you just gave up.' I've finished putting the doona cover on and I'm doing up buttons at the bottom.

'I'm sorry,' Noah says.

'Did you like playing football?'

'Yeah. I always had fun playing. But in year seven I started getting bigger and people started teasing me. And Dad goes on and on about kilojoules in and kilojoules out, but it's not that simple. I've *tried* eating less but it never works.'

Maybe everything isn't that simple, but some things are.

'Even if you don't want to do sport, please stop smoking,' I say. I feel like I might cry.

'What? I don't smoke.'

'But you said everyone does in high school?'

'Most people try it, but smoking is not exactly ideal for trumpet players, you know.'

'That's good,' I say. 'One less thing to worry about.'

'Do you worry about me?'

'No,' I say. But he knows I do.

'Listen,' he says. 'You don't have to worry about me. Yeah, I miss playing footy, but I've got other stuff I like doing too. I have friends and trumpet and … other things. I really am fine.'

He smiles at me, and I actually believe my big brother this time.

I spread the doona across the bed and we both tug on the sides to smooth it down. Noah puts the pillows against the headboard.

I wonder what Noah meant by 'other things'. Maybe he has a girlfriend. Or a boyfriend. He would never tell me, but I will keep an eye out for signs.

Noah goes outside to pick flowers to put on the bedside table. I go to my room and take the agate crystal out from under my pillow. I put it in the drawer beside Mum's side of the bed.

Nana is right. Everything feels better with fresh sheets.

When Mum gets home she goes straight to her bed to lie down. She really appreciates how Noah and I decorated her room, particularly how we folded two towels into the shape of a swan based on a video on the internet. Noah says our swan looks more like a diseased vulture, but Mum is pleased with it, which is what counts.

In the afternoon, Mum gets up and we play Monopoly. Mum wins as per usual because she has more business sense than the rest of us or, as Noah says, she's a filthy capitalist.

Nana cooks a casserole for tea.

After dinner, Dad and I pack the dishes into the dishwasher together. 'What a wild week,' he says.

'Yeah.' He's right, it's been hectic.

'I'm worried that you might have been a bit forgotten in all the fuss about Mum,' he says.

'No one forgot me. Nana picked me up from school.'

'I don't mean literally forgotten. But do you

remember what you said in Doctor Stanford's office?' he asks.

'Which bit?' But I know what he's talking about.

'When you said you didn't think there was a point in being alive if you can't run.'

My eyes fill with tears because I did say that. 'I didn't mean it. I was being dramatic.'

'You're going through a very hard thing,' says Dad. 'Sometimes when people go through things like that, they think about hurting themselves. Is that something you've been thinking about?'

'No. Not properly.' I'm crying. 'It's just that I had nothing to look forward to anymore.'

'Do you feel that way now?' asks Dad.

'No.'

'Do you promise you'll tell me if you feel like that again?' asks Dad. He has stopped packing the dishwasher and is facing me.

I keep facing the bench, stacking the plates into a pile. 'Probably.'

'Why only probably?'

'I don't want to make you upset.'

'I might feel upset, but that's okay. You're more important than me being upset.'

I look up at him and see that he's crying, but I understand this time. I hug him, and I hope we both feel better soon.

*

On Friday after school, Nana picks me up and we go straight home. Mum's having a sleep, so Nana gets out her cards and we play patience at the table. It's relaxing to have busy hands. Patience is not a very hard game. Nana and I chat while we play.

She tells me about her new book club. She doesn't like it much because the ladies drink too much wine and never read the books.

'What do you talk about then?' I ask.

'The climate crisis, the size of bananas, Syria.' Nana stands up suddenly. 'That reminds me,' she says. She walks over to the sideboard and picks up a letter. 'This came for you.' She hands me an envelope.

I rip it open. It's from Radio 3PT. I got an interview for the cadetship!

'What is it?' asks Nana, so I explain about the cadetship.

Noah comes into the room as I'm explaining.

'Congratulations,' he says.

I shrug.

'It's about time we had some good news,' says Nana. 'Now, I need to go check on the washing.'

'You don't seem very excited about this radio thing,' Noah says.

'Would you be? It's just the community radio station.'

'It could be fun. And they have *The Sports Report*. That show's hilarious.'

'I thought you hated sport?'

'I do not, and *The Sports Report* is different anyway.'

'I don't know if I want to do it.'

'Why?'

'It's a waste of time.'

'You're *not* going to keep running, are you?'

I don't say anything for a moment, but finally I say, 'No.' It's true this time.

'Then you need to find something else to think about.'

'I wouldn't be any good on the radio.'

'Yes, you would. Sometimes you actually make mindless boring sport sound kind of interesting.'

'You hate my running stories!'

'Sometimes I hide my true opinions.'

'Alright, if I do the radio station you have to start playing footy again.'

'What's it got to do with me?'

'You love playing – you're just worried about what other people think about you. That's a crap reason to stop doing something.'

Noah seems to be thinking hard. And then he nods. It's a deal.

*

On Wednesday, Alex wants to speak to me before school. Olivia goes over to the basketball courts to find Liza, and I sit down on the bench near the front gate next to Alex.

'Grade fives have sports today, Vivian,' he says.

'Yeah, I know.'

'Are you going to come this time?'

I shrug. 'Maybe.'

'I really want you to,' he says. 'There's lots of things you can do. And we miss you when you're not there. Some of the others take games a bit too seriously. You lighten things up.'

'Sure, I'll come.' It's not like I want to spend every Wednesday watching Matt do his marking.

'I just don't want to catch you running sprints again,' says Alex.

I thought I was feeling better about giving up running. But when Alex mentions sprints, I remember the feeling of running fast, and that's all I want to do. Suddenly I feel almost crushed with disappointment all over again.

'So – is that an agreement?' says Alex.

I can't reply because I feel like I'm going to cry.

'Listen,' says Alex. 'This is going to be tough for you. I'm not going to lie. You are a talented runner and you've had a big setback. Believe me, I know this is disappointing for you, probably more than most people. But, mate, this is a marathon, not a sprint.'

'What do you mean?' Suddenly I have hope that Alex has a plan to get me into marathon running.

'Some days, you're going to feel better, other days worse. That's okay, you just have to hang in there.'

I nod. It's disappointing that the marathon is just a metaphor, but I think I understand what Alex means.

'One more thing,' says Alex. He reaches into his black backpack and pulls out a long object wrapped in paper. 'This arrived yesterday. They finally had it engraved.' He hands the package to me.

I unwrap the paper. Inside is a trophy. On top is a statue of a girl running. Her body is silver and her singlet, shorts and ponytail are bronze. She's on top of a blue column, and when it catches the light, I see flecks of rainbow colour. The base is made of white marble with a gold plaque that reads:

Girls Eleven-Year-Old
Loddon Mallee Region
Cross Country Champion
Vivian Hassler

I stare at it for a long time. When I glance back at Alex, he looks blurry.

'You earned it,' says Alex. He's smiling, but then he says, 'Don't cry! Or I will too.'

I realise that Alex actually is disappointed for me too. I had a bit of ability, and that matters to him.

I wrap the trophy up again and put it in my bag, feeling sadder and better at the same time. Then I walk over to the basketball courts where Olivia and Liza are waiting.

'What did Alex want?' asks Olivia.

'You know, just the usual lecture about not running.'

I tell them about the cadetship at 3PT Community Radio.

'Is that your dream now?' asks Olivia. 'To be a journalist?'

It's too soon to say, so I just shrug.

The song *When I Grow Up* starts playing, and it's time to go to class. Liza stands up and says, 'Come on, Team Olizian.'

'What?'

'Olizian,' repeats Liza. 'I thought that could be our new name.'

For a moment, I think that Olivia is going to argue, but then she says, 'Okay.'

After our soccer warm-up we play a game and Alex says that I can be goalie. It's better than being the umpire so I don't complain.

Liza is dominating the game, and she's on my team, so most of the time I don't have much to do. Alex probably planned it this way.

I'm looking up at the sky, when suddenly I hear Olivia yelling, 'Vivian!' I look across and see Sam dribbling the ball towards me. Olivia is chasing after him, but I don't think she can catch up. Sam is running and looks very determined. Part of me wants to get out of his way, but I don't. I stand in the middle of the goal and watch the ball. Sam kicks and I make a choice. I leap to the left and catch the ball in mid-air.

Sam puts his hands on his head but then smiles. 'Nice one,' he says.

Liza and Olivia come over and we all high five each other.

Olivia tightens her ponytail and says, 'Let's go, Team Olizian,' then runs back to the centre.

Once again, the ball is down the other end of the field and I've got nothing to do except think. The next Olympic Games will be on soon. It will be hard to watch the athletes trying their hardest and the crowds cheering for them. I remember the spectators cheering as I crossed the line at the regional cross country final. It hurts to think that will never happen to me again – but lots of other things will. Things are always changing, and I am too.

Maybe I can still go to the Olympics – not as a spectator, but as a sports journalist. Or maybe Olivia will find a cure for long QT syndrome in time for me to compete in the Olympics. And I still haven't tried archery. There's a chance I might be really good at that.

I don't know what will happen, but if my heart keeps going, I'll find out.

ACKNOWLEDGEMENTS

Thank you to everyone at UQP for publishing this book, particularly Cathy Vallance and Clair Hume. Working with editor Melissa Keil for the first time has been a delight. I am also grateful to Kristina Schulz for her belief in my writing, her professional advice and her kindness.

Caroline Martin provided valuable input on an early draft of the manuscript. Siti (Z) Najla gave very useful feedback on this manuscript and help with many other things.

Liam Delany's expertise on running and living vigorously are a big part of this book and I would like to thank him for always telling me I could have gone harder.

I am grateful to Julie Weir for information about

long QT syndrome and for her enthusiasm about the manuscript. Liz Potter helpfully discussed medical aspects of long QT syndrome with me in the early stages of writing.

Tangeys Marilyn, Peter, Georgina, Mary-Anne and Bonnie read the story and gave me useful feedback and corrections. I would also like to thank them for letting me believe I would be an Olympic athlete until I worked out the truth for myself.

My friends supported me during a rough time when I wrote the first draft of this book. I hope the Barcelona Olympics theme song, '*Amigos para Siempre*', is true for us. Jo Rosenberg, Nerida Lloyd, Bronwyn Tracey and Vaya Pashos – like Australia's 1992 gold medallists – you should all get a Golden Holden.

This story was partly inspired by my cousin Jacinta Laird and her family. Jacinta shared her knowledge of living with long QT syndrome and I am very grateful for her generosity.

And lastly, thank you to Lincoln, Leo and Nina for being my family.

Also by Penny Tangey
STAY WELL SOON

Notable Book CBCA Book of the Year for Younger Readers
Shortlisted NSW Premier's Literary Awards
Shortlisted Western Australian Premier's Book Awards
Shortlisted Readings Children's Book Prize

Stevie has a lot of dreams ... more friends at school, better drawing pencils and a pony. If only she had her dream horse, her life would be better and the other horse-mad girls would talk to her.

When her brother is taken to hospital, Stevie's dreams seem further away than ever. Suddenly her after-school world is filled with hospital visits and there's even less money for anything, especially a pony.

With Stevie's mum spending more time with her brother, Stevie has to learn to figure out the hard things in life by herself.

'A beautiful novel about the fine line between life and death. This is a book which will stay with you long after the final word is read.' *Children's Books Daily* blog

'A gem of a book.' *Australian Book Review*

ISBN 978 0 7022 4994 5

UQP